Beneath
the Boards

David Haynes

Edited by
Storywork Editing Services

Cover Design by
James, GoOnWrite

Formatting by
Polgarus Studio

To find out more about David Haynes and his books
visit his website

http://davidhaynesfiction.weebly.com/

or follow him on twitter
@Davidhaynes71

For Sarah and George

1

Stokes knocked on the door and waited. Four unanswered phone calls and three unreturned text messages had left him with no choice.

"Just answer the door," he whispered.

Natalie Sutton was a mess. In almost every part of her life she had, at one point or another, made the wrong decision.

Do you want to start smoking cannabis at thirteen, Natalie? *"Yes, sir."*

Do you want to have a baby at fourteen, Natalie? *"Yes, please."*

Do you want to have another baby at sixteen, Natalie? *"Of course! Who wouldn't?"*

What about starting a relationship with a man twice your age? He's a real catch; he's beaten every woman he ever knew to a bloody pulp. *"Oh, go on then, if you insist."*

He exhaled loudly and banged on the door. "Natalie? It's DC Stokes, can you open the door please?"

He knew she was in. He'd had a quick look through the lounge window on his way up the driveway. The TV was on and kids' toys lay strewn about. There was even a half-eaten chocolate biscuit on the carpet.

He crouched and pushed the letterbox open. "Natalie, I only want to ask you a quick question, that's all. Just open up and I'll be out of your hair in two minutes."

He'd worked in the Domestic Violence Unit for the last eight years and in that time he'd investigated just about every crime imaginable. He'd also dealt with the unimaginable ones too.

'*High Risk*' – that was the designation given to the victims he worked with. These were the women who appeared on the front page of the newspaper when they'd been murdered by their devoted boyfriends, husbands and lovers. These were the women he wanted to protect.

He had six other women on his workload and they all needed his help, but there was high risk and then there was Natalie Sutton. She courted violence; she sought it out wherever and in whomever she could. He'd been visiting her for the last six months, trying to make her see, trying to make her understand that there was another way to live. He'd backed her when the other agencies wanted to close the door on her and take the baby into care. He believed in her and he believed he was right.

He walked back to the lounge window and cupped his hands around his face. For a brief moment he looked into his own eyes and saw seventeen years of policing staring back at him. It wasn't a pretty sight.

The room was the same as it had been just a couple of minutes ago. The half-eaten biscuit, the beaker lying on its side with a purple stain spreading across the carpet. Someone ought to clean that up before it...

The smashed mobile phone.

The cracked television screen and a thin mist of blood up the wallpaper.

Stokes unclipped his radio and lifted it to his mouth. "NA, this is DC Stokes. Can I have another unit to join me at 18 Scarsdale, please?"

"Received. What have you got?"

Stokes walked quickly to the front door and tried the handle. It didn't move an inch.

"Not sure. Send someone with the big key."

"Received. One unit en route to you now."

There were times when things weren't exactly as they first appeared and there were times when they were spot on, or as near as damn it. He'd been a copper long enough to know this was the latter.

The intelligence on Natalie was that she was in a relationship with Shane Young. He was a nasty, violent shit and Stokes had sent him to court seven years ago for trying to demolish his previous partner's face with a hammer. Shane Young was not the right man for Natalie Sutton, not now, not ever.

He ran around the side of the house and pushed open the wooden gate. The backyard was a mixture of dog crap, abandoned dolls and rotting marrow bones. The smell was powerful but nothing new, nothing out of the ordinary.

"Natalie!" he called out.

Stokes paused at the patio door and unclipped his baton from the covert harness. He'd been bitten by both dogs and humans before and it was nasty. A sight of the baton usually calmed...

A smear of blood and handprints on the inside of the patio doors which were slightly ajar.

"NA from DC Stokes."

"Go ahead."

"There's blood inside the property and signs of disturbance. What's the ETA for uniform?"

"They're en route. Do you need them to come code blue?"

"Yes." He kept his voice as level as he could but already the adrenal gland was doing what it did best.

How long could he stand there waiting for assistance? He should wait, he knew he should. He should stand down and wait for the uniform lads to come with their wailing sirens and stab-proof vests. But he couldn't and he wouldn't.

He gripped the plastic handle and slid the door open.

"Natalie? Are you okay?" He cocked the baton over his shoulder and listened. There was nothing, not even the sound of a two year old playing. He glanced at the blood on the door and stepped further into the room. It smelled of stale cigarette smoke and blood. It smelled of violence.

The kitchen door was off the lounge, just beside the patio doors and he stepped toward it. The kitchen was an arsenal for someone with the wrong mentality. However he was feeling, he needed to check the rooms systematically, starting with the kitchen. He took another step and froze.

He could hear the sound of a child crying upstairs. It wasn't a full heartbreaking howl but it was a forlorn whimper. It was the sound of a child used to being ignored; the sound of a child who knew nobody would come however long she cried.

He needed to get up there quickly, before any more blood was spilled. Natalie was vulnerable enough but the little girl needed taking out of this situation. Whatever had happened here, whatever was happening here was toxic and it was time to put a stop to it. His heart was beating like a drum and although he'd been in these situations before, it never felt good. It never felt right.

He took a step forward, toward the hallway and the little baby upstairs when a great roar sounded from behind him. He turned just in time to see the snarling face of Shane Young smash into his own face and knock him backward.

The kitchen. He hadn't checked it.

The little girl had disturbed him before he'd had a chance to check properly. His eyes immediately filled with tears and for a moment his vision was gone. It was enough time for Young to drive a fist into his face and knock him and his baton to the grubby carpet.

As soon as he hit the floor, Stokes rolled to the side. He couldn't see anything but he was damned if he was going to make it easy for Young. He just had to last long enough for the uniform to arrive.

"I've always wanted to do a pig."

Stokes blinked and cleared his vision enough to see Young coming toward him with a knife in his hand. He looked around for the baton but it had rolled to the other side of the room in the initial assault. He still had his gas but there wasn't enough time to unclip it, let alone point and spray it. Think fast, Stokesy, think fast.

He rocked onto his knees and lunged forward, colliding with Young's shins. The move shocked the other man and he stumbled backward and went down. As soon as he landed, Stokes drove one of his own fists into Young's nose, sending an arc of blood over them both.

Young yelped and tried to push the knife toward Stokes's neck but he batted it away easily, sending it skidding across the threadbare carpet. He drew back his fist and punched the man again and this time the fight went out of Young completely. Stokes reached into his harness and pushed the red button on the top of his airwave radio.

"More units to 18 Scarsdale!" he shouted.

A mixture of sweat and blood dripped off the end of his nose and landed on Young's cheek. Even though the fight had lasted only a matter of seconds, he was exhausted and already his muscles were aching.

He unclipped his cuffs and rolled Young onto his side. "I'm arresting you on suspicion of assault, Shane. You do not have to say…"

"What have you done to him?"

Stokes looked up into the bloodshot and bruised eyes of Natalie Sutton. "Are you all right, Natalie?"

She stared back at him. "If you've hurt him I'll…" Her words were distorted to the point of being almost unrecognisable. Her chin was covered in blood and her vest was a crimson bib. She opened her mouth to say something else, revealing two missing teeth and another which dangled precariously.

"Why didn't you answer my calls?" Stokes finished handcuffing Young and rose slowly to his feet. Forty-three was too old to be fighting with anyone and every inch of his six-foot frame ached to the point of pain. He'd feel this for the next week.

Natalie looked down on her boyfriend and started to cry. "Look what you've done to him. He said you lot were bullies and…"

Stokes took her gently by the shoulders. "Did he do this to you, Natalie?" She looked vacantly at him. It was the look of someone who had nothing, nothing at all.

"Nat…?"

The searing pain in his side stopped him in his tracks. At first he thought might be having a heart attack but the pain was much lower than that. It was somewhere beneath his ribcage. He gasped and tried to steady his breathing.

It was probably just a bad stitch, he really ought to start going to the gym again. Maybe after today he…

He looked down and saw a red bloom spreading across his white shirt. Instinctively he dropped a hand and touched the cotton – it was warm and sticky. Natalie's lost and desperate eyes met his own and as he opened his mouth to ask her why he was bleeding, a second burst of terrible pain exploded in his side. It squeezed every molecule of air from his lungs.

"Do it babe, do it again!" The sound of Young's shrill voice echoed in the room. Stokes caught sight of Natalie's arm thrusting forward again. This is it, he thought, and allowed his legs to collapse under him. Gutted by someone I was trying to protect. The irony of it all.

The sirens screeched and then squealed in the distance and the child upstairs screamed in perfect harmony.

2

Stokes turned the key and pushed the door open with his foot. The hinges creaked like the bones of a tired old man. He waited for a moment and stepped inside. Never again would he cross a threshold, any threshold, without feeling that someone was waiting for him on the other side. He touched his t-shirt just above the scar. "New start, Stokesy. New start."

Light flooded into the room from the French Doors and he walked over and looked out. Lake Stormark looked grey and lifeless in the late-afternoon light. It was completely deserted except for a flock of geese that ran along the shoreline cackling at each other. Stokes watched them until they disappeared from his sight. The cottage was nearly two hundred miles away from his old life but it might as well have been on another planet.

"Everything all right, Mr Stokes?"

He jumped and turned around. He'd forgotten about the estate agent.

"Fine. Everything's fine." The words tripped off his tongue like a well-rehearsed line from a script.

She took a step into the house. "You won't find a view like that very often."

Stokes didn't need to turn around again. This was his fifth visit to the place and his first as more than merely a visitor. The view had been imprinted on his mind after the first visit.

"The spares, I told you I'd find them." She tossed a bunch of keys across the room at him. "I'm not sure you'll ever have to lock the door though. Not around here."

"Thanks, thanks for everything." He wanted her to leave now. Not because he disliked her but because he wanted to be alone with the house for the first time. It belonged to him now.

An awkward silence developed before the estate agent turned away. "I hope you'll be happy here, Mr Stokes."

"I hope so too." This time he meant exactly that. He wanted to feel happy again and this little place was the key to it, he was sure.

He pushed the door shut behind the estate agent and locked it. He might not have to lock the door but he needed to, each and every time.

"New start, Stokesy. New start." If he repeated the mantra enough times it was bound to stick at some point. The words bounced off the empty walls and crashed into each other, jumbling them up. They were meaningless unless he really meant it and although he might want to believe it was a new start, it wasn't. Not quite yet anyway.

He slid his back down the door and sat on the floor. One year. One year to the day since he'd been inside that house. One year to the day since he'd been sliced open and felt the agony of cold steel cut through his body as if it were made of nothing more than jelly. Instinctively he reached inside his t-shirt and touched the scar. Three inches of new, raised skin, that was all there was to show for it. Nobody would ever know it was there and yet it ached each and every day. Each and every day the ache reminded him of what had happened. And with each passing day, the scar grew. Not on the outside where everyone could see it and understand it, but on the inside, inside his mind. You couldn't patch that up. You couldn't stitch that up with a surgeon's needle and thread any more than you could fix Natalie Sutton's life. Some things were just meant to be and somehow or other you just had to get used to it. You had to live with it.

"This carpet has got to go." He jumped up. The floral pattern wasn't him, he wasn't sure it was anyone really. He looked around the room, the only room, downstairs. There was a fair bit of work to do to make it a home, his home. He rubbed his hands together, just as he'd seen his dad do when faced with a serious job. That suited him fine. A bit of DIY was just what the doctor ordered.

Well, that wasn't quite right, the doctor had actually ordered a dose of anti-depressants and rest, but what the hell did he know? Not a lot as it happened. What he really needed was a proper doer-upper by the lake in the middle of nowhere and a very early retirement on a full pension.

That was apt to put a smile on your face. At least for a while.

There weren't many items of furniture which fit in with the 'new start' regime but the black leather recliner was one of them. He put his back against it and shoved it across the carpet toward the French Doors. The only reason it had survived the lifestyle cull was because it felt like it was made for the lake house, made for parking right in front of the doors and reclining on. It had been designed exclusively for staring across the lake while trying desperately not to think about the way the knife felt as it slipped through his body.

He pulled the doors open and collapsed into the chair. It might be another week until the new bed arrived but he had a feeling it wouldn't get much use. He pulled the lever and raised the leg support. A cool breeze washed over him and carried with it the sounds of geese and the pine trees stretching their long slender necks on the far side of the lake. One day he'd forget about Natalie and all the sordid violence that went hand in hand with her life because that's what was supposed to happen. Eventually it would happen, eventually.

He lifted a hip flask from his jacket and raised it to the lake. "Here's to you, Stokesy. And here's to your new start." He put it to his lips and took a sip of Scotland's finest.

He slipped it back inside his pocket and pulled his jacket around his body. He'd get up and close the doors shortly but for now he wanted to listen to the sound of the

world going about its business without humans
interfering.

*

Someone was poking him with a stick and the sharpened
point was right on his scar. There wasn't much pressure at
the moment but it was increasing slowly. He flinched and
tried to push it away but his hand slipped through it as if
it wasn't there. How could that be? He could feel the cool
wood against his skin as it made a small indentation above
the scar. He kicked out again. Who was trying to hurt him
like this? He couldn't see through the fog, but he wasn't
just going to let it happen, not again. He put his head
down and ran as fast as he could but his legs didn't seem
to want to move and the point of the stick was scratching
him now, picking away at the doctor's finest stitches and
teasing them out. He had to stop it happening and he had
to do it before the stick broke the surface and everything
came tumbling out in a terrible crimson tangle. He kicked
out again and shouted…

Stokes's body jerked violently, sending him hurtling
back into the world of the living. His eyes took a moment
to focus and his brain even longer to play catch-up. He felt
cool, not cold, just a little bit on the wrong side of
comfortable. He stretched his back and rotated his neck. It
looked suspiciously like dawn was breaking over the lake.
He checked his watch. It was just after six-thirty. Had he
really slept the whole night through on the recliner? In the
half-light he could see dark shadows darting across the

surface of the lake as the birds caught their breakfast. He knew the answers to the questions. It must have been the fresh air that sent him into such a heavy sleep. He couldn't recall the last time he'd managed three hours unbroken rest, let alone a whole night.

He needed a cup of tea and he cursed himself for not unpacking the box labelled 'unpack me first' last night. He slid off the recliner and stretched his back again. It didn't feel as bad as he'd feared, not as stiff as it should feel anyway. He grabbed the oversized box and hauled it into the kitchen. He'd only brought two boxes with him and one contained clothes. This was the only one with anything of value in it.

He untucked the flaps and grabbed the kettle, the milk, the tea bags and the single mug from inside. There was also a toaster, a four-pack of baked beans, a pack of butter and some bread inside. That would all come later though. Right now he needed a good strong cup of tea and then he'd see about some food.

The cottage was no poster-boy for a modern homes magazine, but it had electricity and a grubby-looking fridge and that was just about right for Stokes. In fact he'd paid extra to keep the fridge because it looked like it might become an icon at some point in the next couple of years.

He poured boiling water into the mug and looked across the open-plan space. It wouldn't take much to turn it into a real stunner and in winter the wood burner would kick out enough heat to warm the place through, if he could find a source of logs. Although it might be therapeutic to chop his own logs. He pushed at the carpet with his feet and stamped down. Once the carpet was up, the floorboards, if they were still serviceable, would need sanding down and waxing. He'd done it before, it was laborious and time-consuming but so what? He had all the time in the world.

He finished making the tea and took his mug back to the open doors. It was absolutely idyllic. Maybe he would get used to leaving doors open after all. Not just yet though. He pulled them closed.

It was only about twenty feet to the shoreline and as a gaggle of Canada geese waddled across in front of him, he held up his mug. "Morning ladies."

The bird at the front of the troupe stopped and all the others followed suit, stopping in a neat line behind her. The brown and black feathers of the birds fluttered in the breeze.

"Can I help you?" Stokes asked. Perhaps he might start throwing bread out for them now and again, they were quite appealing as long as they kept their distance.

One by one the geese slowly turned their slender black necks and looked at him. He counted them. There were fifteen in all and they were all staring at him. Their chatter had stopped and for a moment it seemed so surreal that Stokes thought he was still dreaming. Then all hell broke out.

The lead goose turned on the one behind and grabbed its neck, twisting it so the goose was forced down onto the sandy foreshore. The others rounded on the prone bird and started driving their beaks into it. Stokes watched open-mouthed as the bird was tossed into the air, not once but several times. Blood sprayed in a fine mist and then showered the birds, turning their feathers a deeper shade of brown. Plumage fluttered through the cool morning air like autumn leaves and fell silently onto the lake.

The geese honked triumphantly as their fellow flock member lay dead at their webbed feet. Slowly, as one they turned their dripping beaks toward Stokes and hissed, sending an aerosol of blood toward him. He instinctively stepped back although there was no danger of it reaching him.

What the hell was that all about? It was almost as if they wanted him to watch the carnage, as if it had been a show especially for him. They turned away as one and waddled off along the shoreline and out of view. Stokes grimaced. Was it some sort of territory thing? Or perhaps a show of strength? Whatever it was, 'hideous' came close to describing it. The dead bird's blood, what was left of it, leaked slowly into the water and spread across the lake like an oil slick.

He looked down at the bird. A fox would probably come along and take care of it and if it didn't then he'd just have to go down and push it into the lake. It was just a natural incident and things like that probably happened all the time, he'd just never lived out in the sticks before. Nevertheless his heart was beating a lot quicker than it ought to and he recognised anxiety when it crept through his veins. He looked away. It had unnerved him, that was all.

Now, what was the first job? Unpacking probably, but that would only take as long as it took to plug the toaster in and put the milk and butter in the fridge. He might stretch to carrying the box of clothes upstairs but tipping them onto the floor was a step too far. What was it the ex-Mrs Stokes had said? *"Jim, one day you'll get home late from work again and all your clothes will be in a box on the front lawn."* But she'd left long before Natalie had slipped a knife inside his guts, long before he'd packed his own clothes inside a cardboard box and left.

The bedroom was as bare as the rest of the house and he dropped the box in the middle of the room. Two skylights had been cut into the roof, affording a view of the far side of the lake and the thick covering of pine trees beyond. There was not another house to be seen. It was the same country but it felt like another world from the one he'd just left.

The sound of fist on wood stopped any chance he'd had of slipping into a daydream. Someone was at the door. He didn't have to answer it if he didn't want to, there was no requirement to be friendly or welcoming.

"Hello!" a voice called. "Are you in there?"

Stokes bit his lip.

"Hello? Mr Stokes, I've baked you a cake!"

How did, whoever it was, know his name? That was all he needed, some busybody poking about in his business. He walked slowly downstairs and opened the door. To his relief there was nobody there. They must have got fed up with waiting.

A loud tapping came from behind him and he jumped. "Hello!"

Stokes turned to see a small plump figure standing at the French Doors. She was grinning like a Cheshire cat and holding a cake tin in her hands.

"I've baked you a cake," she said superfluously.

Stokes smiled and walked over. He opened the doors. "Hello?"

"Oh how nice to finally meet you, Mr Stokes! My husband said I should wait a day or two but I'm afraid I couldn't contain myself." She handed the cake tin to him. It felt as heavy as a rock.

"I'm sorry, who are you?"

She peered around his body. "Not unpacked yet, I see."

"Not yet," Stokes replied a little curtly.

"Oh I am sorry. I'm Ina, Ina Gauchment and I'm your neighbour."

He put the cake tin down by his feet. It would act as a barrier to discourage her from coming in, he hoped.

He held out his hand. "Jim Stokes, pleased to meet you."

"Ah Jim is it? Short for James, I assume? We were all wondering what your first name was." She tried to look over his shoulder but Stokes shifted his weight. "And Mrs Stokes, is she in?"

"No, she popped out for bread," he lied.

A moment of awkward silence followed. Ina Gauchment clearly thought the cake would secure her entry. Stokes had other ideas.

"Well, Mrs Gauchment, I've got a lot to be getting on with. As you've seen I haven't even unpacked yet."

"Ina. It's Ina." She looked disappointed and for a second Stokes considered inviting her in. It was only a second though.

"Well, it was lovely meeting you and thanks again for the cake. I'll see you again sometime." He started to close the door but she thrust her hand inside.

"Oh but you'll see us all at the gathering tonight, won't you?"

What the hell was the gathering? "Sorry?"

"You'll be coming, of course."

"I'm afraid not. I'll still be unpacking. Some other time."

"Unpacking two boxes won't take long, Jim. Besides if you don't come and meet everyone, I'll bring them here to meet you. Seven o'clock sharp at the hall." She pointed over his shoulder. "Five minutes down the road there."

This was his worst nightmare. No that wasn't right, he'd lived his worst nightmare for the last year but this came a valiant second.

"I really can't, Mrs… Ina. I'm not one for things like that. I'm antisocial to be honest."

"Oh what rot! Of course you can. Mrs Stokes will love it, I'm sure."

"Mrs Stokes?" He forgot his lie.

"Your wife?" She turned away. "Seven o'clock sharp or we'll be marching up here to bang on your door." She started toward the side of the house and suddenly stopped.

"What happened to that goose?"

Stokes shrugged. "A domestic, I think."

"Do you want it?"

"Want it? No." He was confused.

"Waste not, want not." Ina marched toward the shoreline and grabbed the goose by its bloody neck. She examined it briefly before slinging it over her shoulder. She waved with her free hand and walked along the shoreline.

"Everyone's really looking forward to meeting you, Jim!" A crimson smear painted the rear of her smock.

Stokes stared at the space where Ina had been a few moments before. He felt like he'd just been caught up in a whirlwind. At least she'd got rid of the goose, she'd thrown it over her shoulder as if it was an everyday occurrence.

"Waste not, want not, Stokesy."

He'd have to go to this gathering, whatever it was. It was either that or have a whole gaggle of busybodies turn up at his door demanding to meet him. He would show his face for half an hour and come away. Mrs Stokes might be having a bad turn tonight, a migraine or something, and he couldn't possibly stay any longer.

3

Stokes followed the lane into the village, such as it was. There were no more than five or six houses spaced evenly along the lane and although Ina had said she was a neighbour, there were no houses closer than a ten minute walk away from his own. Knowing that made him feel a little better.

"Mr Stokes?"

A man waved to him up ahead. He was standing in the middle of the road, beaming. Stokes held up his own hand and tried to smile. The man walked toward him with his hand out.

"Mr Stokes, great to meet you. Peter Gauchment." He took Stokes's hand and pumped it hard. His untidy mop of curly, steel-grey hair wobbled with enthusiastic vigour. "Have you come for the gathering?"

"Jim Stokes. Your wife more or less threatened me. I can't stay long though, I'm afraid." He was already making his excuses to leave early.

Peter Gauchment dropped the handshake and patted him on the back. "Well, we better get you inside to meet everyone then!"

Peter led him along the road to the last building in the village. A neat wooden sign hung at the apex of the roof: 'Stormark Village Hall'.

"Here we are."

Peter practically shoved him through the door. Immediately Ina was upon him, grabbing his shoulders and planting a kiss on his cheek.

"How lovely to see you, Jim. I wasn't sure you'd come."

Stokes pulled away. "Did I have a choice?"

Ina took his arm. "Choice? No of course you didn't." She peered over his shoulder for the second time that day. "And Mrs Stokes?"

Stokes was on the verge of lying again but he decided truth was a better option, particularly if he intended on staying in Stormark.

"I'm afraid I told a little fib about that. Mrs Stokes, at least the former Mrs Stokes, is living somewhere in Derbyshire with her new man. That is to say there is no Mrs Stokes, not any more."

Ina waved her hand dismissively. "Oh I know that, Jim. I know everything about our little village."

Stokes didn't doubt it for a minute.

He was shown like an exhibit to everyone else at the gathering. They were a harmless but enthusiastic bunch of middle-aged characters and Stokes found their company to be relatively undemanding.

A pint of warm beer was thrust into his hand by Peter with the exclamation, "I made it myself!"

Stokes sipped it and was pleasantly surprised. "It's very good."

"It ought to be, I've had enough practice. I'll bring some up to you if you'd like?"

Stokes nodded. "Thank you."

Ina pushed Peter out of the way. "Have you tried my Victoria sponge yet?"

"Not yet, Ina."

Her face dropped, she was clearly disappointed.

"But I plan on having a large slice for my supper tonight."

Ina turned away. "Supper? You won't need supper, Jim. Not after you've eaten a Stormark buffet." She disappeared through a door at the rear of the hall.

"I hope you're hungry. She won't be happy if you don't stuff your face, Mr Stokes."

Stokes turned around. A man he hadn't been introduced to yet held out his hand. He looked older than any of the others.

"Edward Willis."

"Jim Stokes. She's quite something, isn't she?"

"Oh yes, she's something all right. Quite what though…" Willis trailed off.

Both men looked about the room in the awkward silence. Stokes sipped his beer.

"Settling in well?" Willis finally asked.

"Only been there just over a day but yes I think so, thank you."

"Good to have someone living up there again. It's been empty too long and a place like that needs someone living in it."

Willis had emphasised the word 'needs' and it hadn't gone unnoticed. "Needs?" Stokes asked.

"Like any house, Mr Stokes, it needs a soul and the soul is provided by the people who inhabit it. A house without anyone living in it is just an empty box, right?"

"Right." Stokes nodded. "It's been empty a while though, at least as far as I know. I've been coming up here looking at it and making my mind up. I've been lucky no-one snapped it up before me."

"Lucky? Perhaps. Only you'll know that though."

"What do you mean?" Stokes was puzzled by the man's cryptic response.

"It's been too long, Mr Stokes. Too long," Willis replied and walked away. After meeting such a friendly and positive group of people, Edward Willis had been quite a bump.

"You've met old grumpy-guts then?"

Peter stood to one side. He smiled but it was thin and without humour.

"He did seem a bit down about something."

"Oh take no notice, he's just a grumpy old bugger." Peter put his arm around Stokes's shoulder and looked around the hall. "Now, who haven't you met yet?"

"I'm pretty sure I've met everyone now." There were

one or two faces he wasn't entirely sure about meeting.

"I was thinking about heading back up the road in a minute or two."

"Come and get it!" Ina shouted from the back of the room.

Peter gave him a shove toward Ina. "Oh you can't possibly leave just yet. Ina has made goose pâté!"

*

Two hours later Stokes did the rounds again, shaking hands with everyone and saying his farewells. Everyone with the exception of Edward Willis, who had clearly managed to make his excuses more effectively than Stokes and left earlier.

"Same time next week, Jim!" Ina shouted from the doorway.

Stokes smiled and waved before walking away. Every week? It seemed excessive but now he'd met everyone he wouldn't have to make an appearance that often. Twice a year seemed about right.

He'd lived in suburbia for his entire life. As a child, he'd grown up in a cul-de-sac and as an adult he'd bought his own house in the comfortable and familiar surroundings of middle-class, middle England. A place where people cut their grass on Saturday and washed their shiny people-carriers on Sunday. A place where nobody got stabbed in the stomach and the street lights stayed on all night.

Stokes put one foot in front of the other. He couldn't

possibly get lost because there was only one road in and out of the village.

But it was dark, so utterly dark. And silent.

Silent except for the occasional screech of an owl which seemed to be following him all the way back home. They weren't all that bad, the Stormark folk. Ina was an acquired taste but she seemed harmless enough, all of them did. And if making the occasional appearance at their gatherings was all it took to placate them then so be it. There were worse things to have to do. There were worse things he'd done.

He clutched a bottle of beer in each hand. Peter's home brew had disappeared earlier on in the evening and someone with less refined taste in beer had clearly brought these two bottles. Nevertheless he intended to sit out by the lake on his own and enjoy every single mouthful. No, this new start had actually started quite promisingly, and most importantly it felt like a different world to Scarsdale Road and all the streets just like all over England.

He opened the door to the cottage and stepped inside. He paused for a moment and took a deep breath. "Hello?" It was a habit he'd tried to break, and although he didn't do it in front of the estate agent, he'd wanted to. He locked the door behind him and walked across the room. The patio doors were locked and the front door had been locked too. No-one could have come in or out and he relaxed.

He'd eaten only a small amount of goose pâté at the gathering but he'd tucked into the rest of the buffet without any such reluctance. The sight of the goose being ripped apart by its comrades flashed through his mind with each bite of the bread. He looked at the cake tin and at the beer in his hands. Now that would make a perfect combination – a couple of beers, a lump of cake and a seat by the lake. He'd have to avoid the goose execution site but there was plenty of room.

He knocked the lid off the beer on the kitchen worksurface and cut an enormous wedge from the cake. This was the life.

The water lapped gently on the sandy foreshore and made a rhythmic scratching noise which was hypnotic. Stokes lowered himself onto the ground and inhaled deeply. The air smelled faintly of pine but the overpowering smell was that of the lake, of water. How did you explain that smell? It was fresh and clean yet somehow of the earth at the same time. Not sterile but not corrupt either, somewhere inbetween, exactly where it should be and it was hugely reassuring.

He looked up at the sky. It was a shame clouds covered the stars. The second or third time he'd come up here, he arrived the night before and slept in his car just so he could meet the estate agent early. He'd come out to the lake, lain on his back on the grass bank and looked up at the stars. It was the first time he'd seen so many and it had been almost too much to comprehend. Had they all just miraculously formed? It seemed impossible that the same stars were always there, even in suburbia.

No such luck tonight though. There was nothing save

for a blanket of darkness overhead. The owl screeched again and Stokes did his best to reply by cupping his hands around his mouth. He waited for a moment but the owl was silent. It was probably disgusted by the rudimentary attempt at conversation. Either that or he'd just said something abusive and the bird had taken umbrage.

"Sorry!" Stokes called.

The beer was nowhere near the standard of Peter's brew but it didn't matter. This was one of those moments where all was well with the world. God knew there hadn't been many of those for a while. He should have made this move months ago, maybe even years ago, before any of that crap had happened.

An occasional pinprick of light wobbled in the darkness. There were houses on the other side of the lake. Some of them were holiday homes, no doubt, and some of them belonged to the residents of a village just like Stormark. The houses were invisible in daylight, covered by the dense woodland, but at night their lights shone out into the darkness like the eyes of some mythical beast.

Tomorrow he'd make a real start on the cottage. At some point he'd have to take the hour-long drive to Mary's Wharf to pick up supplies. He was sure he'd seen a DIY mega-store on one of his many drives through the town too. Sooner or later he'd need to get an additional form of heating into the cottage. The weather was mild enough at the moment but it wouldn't be long until winter arrived and with it sub-zero temperatures. The cottage was beautiful but freezing his nuts off all winter wasn't something he relished.

There was so much to do but there was no rush whatsoever. He rolled onto his stomach. Had he really bought this little piece of heaven? Was it really his?

His heart stopped, or it felt like it had.

Standing on the inside of the cottage, at the patio doors, was Natalie and she held a small silver knife in her bloody hand. He watched breathlessly as a single drop of blood fell from the tip of the blade and landed on the carpet.

"I'll gut you, Stokes." Her mouth was an ugly snarl. She scraped a bloody hand down the inside of the glass, painting a dark smear.

"Natalie?" he whispered. Her face was grey and lined with years of drug and alcohol abuse. But it was her, it was definitely her, there was no mistaking the vapid look of despair in her hazel eyes – despair and spite.

And then she was gone.

Stokes couldn't move. His breathing was short and shallow, and despite the cool night air, a thin sweat had broken out on his forehead. It had been a while but he'd shaken hands with enough panic attacks in the last year to know when one was kicking him in the balls.

Relax and look away, that's what he needed to do, and although Natalie had gone, the outline of her waif-like body remained and it was trying to burn a deep, dark hole into his retina.

"She's not there, Stokes. She's not really there." He bit his lip and flipped over onto his back. The beer splashed over his face but he kept hold of the bottle.

He swallowed hard but most of the moisture had been driven from his mouth. His throat had shrunk down to the size of a pinhead and was filled with jagged razorblades.

He wanted to scream but he'd tried that once before and it hadn't helped that time. Why would it now?

Natalie wasn't there. She had managed to do to herself what Shane Young had been trying to do for the last year – end her miserable life.

"She's not here." Stokes jumped up and turned around. His mind was playing a dirty trick, just reminding him that his life wasn't all beer and skittles. Not quite yet.

There was nobody standing at the glazed doors. There was no dark smear down the glass and nobody was waiting to gut him. He wiped his face and tipped the remainder of the beer into his mouth. One day the ghosts would be banished but it didn't look like they were ready to disappear just yet.

He walked up toward the cottage and peered through the glass. It was dark inside. Tomorrow he'd get a lamp or maybe two. He aimed the torch and directed it around the room until he was satisfied he was safe.

He pushed the doors open and waited for a second.

"Hell…" He stopped short. The beam of the torch had caught something at his feet, something dark and circular in the fibres of the carpet. Something that looked like a drop of blood.

Stokes grunted as a sudden flash of pain exploded in

his side. It drove him to his knees, half-in and half-out of the cottage. The torch rolled away into the centre of the room and the bottle of beer landed with a dull thud on the carpet. His eyes bulged as the terrible agony ripped through his body, crushing his lungs, making it impossible to call out. Not that there was anyone to hear it or come to his aid, but it might have helped.

He'd only felt pain like this once before and that had nearly killed him.

One step at a time, Stokesy.

He dropped onto all fours and shuffled farther into the room, crawling like a baby. Another burst of pain stopped him in his tracks and this time he called out. It was nothing intelligible but it was loud, it was guttural and somehow he thought it might help.

The pain originated from his wound, the long-healed scar which would always remind him of his previous life. He lifted a hand and slipped it under his t-shirt.

It couldn't be opening up again, it was impossible. His fingers felt sticky and wet. They felt warm with blood – his blood. He felt the stinging scratch of the knife as it slipped beneath his skin and cut through his body. He groaned and looked down at his torso. A single droplet of blood clung to his t-shirt long enough for him to see its grip on the cotton give way. As it fell it briefly became a beautiful ruby in the torchlight.

Stokes watched as it made a tiny splash on the carpet before he passed out.

*

"Mr Stokes? Jim, are you all right?"

Stokes was vaguely aware of being cold, and of a numbing sensation of pins and needles all down one side of his body.

"Mr Stokes, can you hear me?"

Where was he? He opened his eyes and the lurid, flowery pattern of the carpet came into focus. He was half-in and half-out of the doorway.

"Jim, I'm going to phone for an ambulance."

Stokes rolled over slowly. "No don't do that, I'm okay." His eyes refocused and the tall figure of Peter Gauchment swam into view. "I'm okay," he repeated.

"What on earth are you doing down there? Did you fall?"

What a ridiculous question. People didn't decide to eat their carpet for fun.

"Must've been that beer of yours." He sat up and rubbed the dead side of his body, the side with the scar. Blood, where was the blood?

His body caught up with his mind and he looked down at his white t-shirt. There was nothing, not a single drop of claret. He slipped his hand under the fabric and ran his fingers across the scar.

"Shit," he hissed through his teeth. The scar was as neatly closed as ever, but it was as tender as it had been immediately after the operation.

"That sounds nasty."

Stokes pulled his shirt back down and raised his hand to Peter. "Give me a hand?"

Peter nodded and pulled him upright. "I've brought you some more." He bent down and picked up a box. "Oh and Ina has put some goose pâté in there too."

Stokes looked down at Peter's feet, at the small brown stain on the carpet. It didn't match the rest of the garish pattern.

"Cheers." He took the box and winced.

"Can I make you a cup of tea, Jim? You look a little green around the gills. I can fetch the doctor if…"

"I'm okay, honestly. I must've just tripped, or something…" He trailed off. Or something.

"You sure? It's no problem, no problem at all."

Like his wife, he appeared desperate to get inside.

"I need to drive over to Mary's Wharf to get some supplies." Stokes patted his pockets for the car keys and his wallet. "Maybe later."

He followed Peter around to the front of the cottage and climbed the steps up to the road.

"You're okay to drive? I wouldn't want any of your colleagues to stop you." Peter smiled.

"Colleagues?"

"The local boys in blue. Although we haven't seen any up here for months."

How did he know about his previous employment? It must have been the estate agent. "Ex," he said shortly.

"I'm sorry?"

Stokes clicked the central locking on the Ford. "Ex-colleagues. I'm not a copper anymore." He opened the door and climbed inside. His body ached and he emitted a grunt as he put the keys in the ignition.

Peter patted the roof. His wedding ring made a metallic chime. "Ah but you know what they say, once a copper always a copper." He grinned broadly and walked toward the village.

"I hope not," Stokes said to himself and pressed the accelerator.

He drove slowly along the quiet lanes toward the town, partly because he still felt groggy and sore, and partly to give himself time to think. He touched his scar again and flinched. It wasn't just sore because of lying on the floor all night, it was tender and raw. It felt like he'd been operated on again. And what of the blood and Natalie's appearance? Had he imagined that? The counsellor had spoken of flashbacks and of events which played over and over again, repeating themselves with perfect clarity until they drove you mad. But who wouldn't have flashbacks when they'd been stabbed? Who wouldn't live every single excruciating moment of that event? It was natural and this was all last night was – a particularly vivid and multi-sensory flashback.

"You have symptomatic post-traumatic stress disorder, Mr Stokes, but we can help alleviate…"

He pushed down hard on the accelerator. The brown stain on the carpet would have to wait until later to be examined. If it was there at all.

*

The boot and back seat were loaded to maximum capacity with an array of items. Groceries sat beside power tools and lamps fell against sheets and duvet covers. Interior design had never been his forte and now it didn't need to be. He only had to please himself and that made things much easier. Once the grim carpet was up, the cottage would be completely pattern-free.

Despite himself, he'd quite enjoyed visiting Mary's Wharf. Nobody knew him and because of that there were none of the well-meant touches on the arm. *"How do you feel?"* or the cringe-worthy, *"I was going to come and see you but..."* The latter was normally from the coppers who didn't want to see what a knife through the guts could do to a man. It was from the guys who thought losing your bottle might be contagious.

The windscreen wipers came on automatically. A slow but persistent fall of rain had started some miles back to accompany the grey skies.

The man at the DIY store had tried to talk him into hiring a floor sander. *"It'll cut the time in half!"* he'd announced. Stokes almost agreed but time wasn't important anymore, so he bought an ordinary belt sander to do the job. It might take a while to get into the frame of mind where he didn't need to rush about, where the passage of time was just something that happened and wasn't an unbeatable opponent.

"Whoa!" Stokes braked hard, narrowly avoiding the

pedestrian walking in the centre of the road. They stared at each other for a moment before Stokes wound down his window.

"Sorry! You okay?" He recognised the other man immediately, it was Edward Willis. "Can I give you a lift?"

Willis wasn't dressed for a stroll in the rain and his hair was plastered down onto his head. Willis took his glasses off and squinted toward the car.

"Mr Stokes? Is that you, Mr Stokes?" He started walking toward the car.

Stokes held up a hand. "Yep." Willis had been utterly downbeat at the gathering and Stokes was pleased it was only a short drive back to Stormark.

Willis climbed inside. "The weather caught me out," he said blandly.

Stokes accelerated. "Good job I nearly flattened you then." His attempt at humour went completely unnoticed.

"Been to town I see. The decoration not to your liking?"

"Just the carpet. I'm not a big fan of 70s patterns."

"Nothing wrong with it in my opinion." Willis stared straight ahead.

Stokes slowed the car as he took a sharp bend. "You've seen it?"

Out of the corner of his eye, he saw Willis turn slightly in the seat.

"Do you know anything about the cottage, Mr Stokes? Anything at all?"

"Nope but the way you've just said that makes me

think I should." He wanted to look at Willis to see what the man's expression was like. All those years of being a detective had taught him how much you could read into someone's face, but the road was too unfamiliar to risk it.

"Perhaps, or perhaps it's irrelevant." His monotonous voice was impossible to read.

"Why don't you tell me and I can decide for myself."

The deep grey of Lake Stormark came into view and with it a glimpse of the cottage.

"You can let me out here. I'll walk the rest of the way." Willis's voice contained a hint of urgency which was amplified due to the man's usual dull tone.

Stokes frowned. "I'll be pulling in just up there, you might as well go that far." He pointed toward the cottage. It was only another few seconds of driving but it would give him time to drag some information from Willis.

"No thank you. Please stop here." He was insistent.

Stokes was frustrated. "And that's it? You're going to leave it there?" He tried not to sound pissed off but he was. When people only gave him half a story, or in this case, a suggestion there might be a story, it usually made him more determined to get them to talk. He pulled the car to a stop.

"I'm sure you'll find out for yourself. Someone with more knowledge on the matter will be happy to tell you." Willis opened the door. "Thanks for the lift."

He watched Willis pull his collars up against the rain and hunch his shoulders over. He didn't need to know anything more about the cottage, especially from a man like Willis. He pulled away and drove the short distance back. It had been a brief encounter with Willis and had done nothing to change his opinion of the man. He was dour and more than a little odd.

Stokes unpacked the supplies and plugged in one of the lamps, which threw out an orange glow. It was a dismal day, even though it was not yet noon. The other one would go in the bedroom when the bed arrived.

He walked over to the patio doors and knelt down. The pattern was terrible and confusing but finding the errant dark spot wasn't difficult. He ran his finger over it. What was he expecting? The warmth of freshly spilled blood or just the crusty spike of an ageing stain? He got neither. The stain seemed to be embedded deep into the fibres of the carpet. It was almost as if it was consuming the blood.

"Don't be ridiculous, Stokes," he muttered.

He'd been back to Scarsdale after the stabbing, not immediately but a safe time later. It had been a time when he thought he might still have a chance of getting through it. If only he could shake off the terrible and constant headaches he might be back at work within a month, two at the most.

The crime scene investigators had cut a hole in the carpet by then and removed any trace of where his body had been found. They had all but eradicated any sign of where his beautiful and pure blood had soaked into filthy carpet, creating just another stain. He'd knelt and run his fingers over the bare floorboards. There was nothing, not even a single droplet of blood had seeped through into the wood. Had he ever been there at all? A smeared hand-print on the pockmarked wall told the story, or part of it. It had been made by a small hand, a woman's hand, smeared in blood. He'd traced his fingers over the outline. The blood had aged badly and turned brown like a cheap, bottom-shelf bottle of red.

He pushed his finger deeper into the pile of the carpet and felt the hard wood of the boards below.

"Shit!" he shouted and withdrew his finger. A pinprick of blood gathered in a ball on his fingertip. He put it in his mouth and sucked it. It was probably just a splinter poking up from the floorboards. He stood up and looked down at the little patch. When he put the belt sander to work there wouldn't be any carpet there, let alone splinters.

4

Stokes tightened the final bolt on the bed and stepped back. Okay, so it was just a bed but he was pleased with it, nearly as pleased as he was with the new partially fitted bathroom suite. They were purely functional items and although he'd quite enjoyed sleeping on the recliner, it was no long-term replacement. His aching back was testament to that. There hadn't been any further flashbacks in the last week. His mind had been too engaged with the vagaries of plumbing to wander into much darker territories.

He stripped the plastic cover from the mattress and heaved it onto the bed. He'd never been addicted to soap operas like the former Mrs S, but he'd still spent a lot of evenings staring inanely into the box. How much time had he wasted doing that? He jumped onto the bed and lay back. It was amazing how much he'd accomplished without the distractions of modern life, without the morbid reminders his brain conjured up.

He looked up at the ceiling. The cottage was old, you just had to look at the thickness of the walls to see that. It had probably gone through countless changes through the decades. Everyone who had lived there had stamped their own signature on it somewhere. There was probably a little piece of each and every former resident in the very fabric of the building.

Apart from fleeting and brief conversations with the delivery drivers, he hadn't seen a soul all week. This was something he'd expected but not totally prepared himself for. It was one thing desiring solitude but another entirely immersing himself in it.

He rolled off the bed and looked out of the Velux window. It was late afternoon and soon lights from across the lake would stab holes in the darkness and drip fire over the water. Would he ever find another partner? Did he want to? His last partnership could hardly be described as a raging success. Four years of marriage and an acrimonious departure for both of them was apt to put anyone off, especially when she worked in the same station. She hadn't come to the hospital to visit him, not that he'd wanted or expected her to, but she had signed the card. Her signature was right in the corner, almost as if it was trying to crawl away and hide somewhere. It was understandable, of course it was, but Melanie was just about the only person who knew what being stabbed would actually do to him.

He turned away and walked back downstairs. It didn't matter anymore, none if it did because he had a new life now.

"Yoo-hoo!" There was no mistaking Ina's friendly voice.

He walked over to the patio doors and smiled. "Hello there." He opened the doors and saw the cake tin in her hands.

"I hope that's not for me." He patted his stomach. "I won't fit into my trousers at this rate."

"Nonsense! You need fattening up. I've come to see if you're coming to the gathering again tonight?"

Had it really been a week since the last one? He hadn't even thought about it. Ina stared at him, exerting a pressure to answer. Would it be so bad? A couple of beers with the folks wasn't such a bad idea. Besides the trip to town, he hadn't been out all week.

"I wouldn't miss it for the world."

The ever-present smile on Ina's face widened a touch. Stokes stepped to the side. "Would you like to come in?" From her reaction last time, he knew she was keen to get in and have a look around.

Her eyes widened for a moment before a frown of confusion spread across her face. "I don't want to be a nuisance."

"You're not." Stokes was puzzled by her reaction. Last week she had practically tried to climb over him to get inside.

"Well, if you're sure." She raised her leg to come over the threshold.

A light thump followed by the sound of smashing glass

came from upstairs. Stokes turned and looked.

"It sounds like you might have a job to do. I'll come back another day, see you later."

Ina had gone before he had the chance to turn back around. He closed the door and went upstairs. The sound had come from the bedroom but he was sure there wasn't any glass in there, apart from the Velux and it didn't sound like a window had been smashed.

At the top of the stairs, he glanced into the bathroom before going into the bedroom. He saw it immediately. The lamp he'd put on the floor beside the bed was lying on its side and glass was scattered around it.

How had the bulb smashed? The shade should stop that happening. He knelt beside it, carefully avoiding the broken glass. One side of the conical shade was crumpled, no that wasn't quite right, it was almost destroyed entirely. Whatever integrity its frame possessed had been removed.

Stokes felt his heart rate quicken. He hadn't left the lamp here, he hadn't left the lamp on the side of the room without a plug socket. Why would he? He pushed the lamp and it wobbled across the glass and into the wall.

The broken glass didn't appear to be in a random pattern. It looked almost… What? It looked ordered. He climbed onto the bed and looked down.

"No?" he whispered.

He was right about the glass, it was ordered all right. It spelled out a word.

"No," he repeated through a mouth that no longer felt like his own.

*

"Great to see you again, Jim." Peter gave him one of his none-too-gentle pats on the back. Despite the number of cakes he must eat, he was in good shape. "Have you recovered?"

"Recovered?"

"Yes, from your fall. You looked quite shaken up."

Stokes had forgotten about Peter's presence in the aftermath. The lead up, however, remained fresh in his memory.

"Fine thanks." He shook Peter's hand. "As I said, that beer of yours is pokey."

Peter laughed and whispered conspiratorially, "I've got some wheat beer that'll knock your socks off, fancy some? You should come over for..." He stopped and looked around the room.

"There she is. Ina, I was just saying to Jim that he should come over for dinner."

Ina rushed over with the trademark smile painted across her ruby-red lips. "What a lovely idea. Friday evening, say seven? We're the last house out of the village, big green door, you can't miss us."

Stokes felt like he'd been run over. "Are you sure? All I seem to be doing is eating your food and drinking your beer."

"Don't be silly. Besides, as you can see, Ina loves cooking."

Stokes looked about the room nodding at people

whose faces he remembered but names he didn't.

"Is Edward Willis here tonight?" he asked.

Ina scuttled off barking an order at one of the others.

"No. He's a grumpy old bugger, no great loss if you ask me." It was the first time Stokes had heard anything but conviviality in Peter's voice.

"I gave him a lift the other day. He wasn't exactly full of the joys of spring then."

"Oh? Where was he?"

"On the road back to Stormark. I saw him as I was coming back from town. It was the same day you found me." A vision of Natalie holding a bloody knife flashed through his mind.

"Yes, our vicar is notoriously surly, but I believe he has a happier side in there somewhere."

"He's the vicar?" Stokes asked. Willis wasn't an archetypal vicar, at least as far as temperament was concerned.

"Well, he used to be, somewhere down south I think. He's retired now of course and we don't have a chapel in Stormark. I'm not sure there's ever been one." Peter looked about the room and waved to someone. "Right, off to circulate."

Stokes stood alone feeling slightly awkward. The incident with the light bulb was still playing out in his mind. He'd swept up the glass and tipped it in the bin but he could still see the word splashed in tiny jewel-like fragments across the floorboards.

Even now he wasn't sure he'd actually seen it. Was it

quite as clear as he remembered? Or was it something his damaged mind had conjured up? He walked to the table and took a bottle of beer. He'd probably left it on the bed and it had simply rolled off, nothing more than that. He took a long draft of the beer and suppressed a belch. The question was, how many of these incidents could he pass off as mischievous tricks played by his mind before he conceded that the doctor might know what he was talking about after all? He took another long drink. He wouldn't go on the tablets again, no way. The cottage was all he needed now and a few weeks of peace would clear his head, he knew it.

He turned and was greeted by an elderly man. "So you were a police officer, Mr Stokes?"

His heart sank. Even when he was a serving officer he preferred to keep it to himself. Requests for advice and the inevitable 'off the record' scenarios made him wary.

"Used to be, yes. Sorry, I've met so many new people recently, I don't recall your name."

"That's all right, it's Jack, Jack Hughes. I always wanted to be a copper, bit too long in the tooth now though. Now then I've got a question for you…"

*

Stokes climbed under the crisp white covers and let out a long drawn-out sigh. It felt good to be in bed. He stretched and pushed his toes against the cool wooden footboard. It made the bed groan in with pleasure.

He could look directly out of the Velux window from

this position and see the stars up above. The moon wasn't visible through his little static viewfinder but a silvery glow indicated its presence in the night sky.

The aftermath of being stabbed had left him unable to sleep, and then eventually when he had slept, it had only been in a room with a light on. That didn't last long though, because the dark corners of his mind could conjure up Natalie whether it was light in the room or not.

He closed his eyes. Tomorrow, all being well, he might make a start on the floor. Pulling up that damn ugly carpet was well overdue. He rolled over onto his front and tried to fill his mind with happy thoughts. He just hoped they were strong enough to keep the bad ones at bay.

*

He stretched his arms and pushed against the headboard. He couldn't remember sleeping quite so well, at least not since the incident. His body ached but it was a pleasant sensation. It was the result of manual labour and his body hadn't grown accustomed to it yet.

Up above, through the window, he could see the sky was a stunning and cloudless azure. He yawned and inhaled deeply. He was used to the metallic smell of the lake and he noticed it less and less each day but this morning it was stronger than normal. It seemed fresher somehow.

A sense of well-being washed over him. He was lucky, lucky to be alive and lucky to find this beautiful cottage in such an idyllic location. Despite the perversities his traumatised mind vomited up, this was definitely going to be the new start he'd hoped for.

He closed his eyes and fell headlong into the moment. Birds settled on the roof and sang a beautiful chorus and in the distance a flock of ducks raced across the surface of the lake trying to take off. Water sprayed from their wing feathers and flew high into the air like ephemeral diamonds. His senses felt amplified. It was almost as if he was part of the ecosystem, not living beside it but within it.

A tingling sensation started in the tips of his toes sending wiry tendrils of pleasure into his calf muscles. The sensation was almost too much to bear.

"Stay," a voice whispered in his ear.

"Stay with me," the soft and feminine voice whispered again. It tickled his ear and he suppressed a shiver.

His eyes were open but the owner of the voice was invisible.

Yet he could feel her. She was in the room with him and there was something about her voice that was sad, almost pathetic.

"I'm staying," he murmured weakly, and he meant it. He never wanted to leave this beautiful place again.

"Stay," her voice was like a fragrant breeze. "Stay," she repeated again and again until he could barely stand to hear the heartbreaking melancholy in her voice.

His body shuddered as an agonising bolt of pain overpowered the pleasure. He roared with distress and sat up. He felt breathless and a thin sweat covered his entire body.

"A dream?" he muttered.

He flopped back down. It might have been a dream but the pain in his side was real. He touched the scar and groaned. Dawn had started to break and the grey morning had enough strength to show the blood on his fingers. It wasn't much but it was there and for whatever reason the scar tissue had opened up just enough to allow a little more of his blood to be spilled.

Accompanying the pain in his body was another sensation though, a thin remnant from the dream. It was strange but he felt a tinge of grief for the owner of the voice, whoever it belonged to.

"Some dream," he whispered.

*

He made coffee and opened the double doors. He'd left the recliner in the same spot since he arrived. It was a couple of feet back from the doors and it afforded a spectacular view of Lake Stormark. He settled into it and pulled a blanket over his legs.

He'd had powerful dreams before. Some good and some not so good but he couldn't ever remember being left with such a strong sense of emotion.

There had been no visual clarity, after all there hadn't been a face to put to the voice, but all the same his senses had been stimulated. His mind was still tingling, albeit the sensation was receding, and the pitch of the voice had already melted away into a recess in his mind. Even the birdsong seemed more doleful than it should. He sipped the coffee and felt the bitter brew send a shuddering buzz through his body. He had no idea how long it would all last but he was going to sit right there and let it wash over him. He'd try to reason it out later, if it needed to be reasoned out at all.

He'd been looking out across the lake while he was considering the dream, allowing his vision to focus on everything and yet nothing at the same time. It was utterly relaxing. But now, as his musing came to a close, he focused on the foreshore. What was that? He got to his feet and leaned forward.

Grey and brown feathers danced about on the breeze and below them, another goose lay slaughtered. Its neck was twisted at an unnatural angle and a dark smear covered its underbelly.

He sat back down and let his eyes drift back to the surface of the lake. Geese could be aggressive, but he'd never seen them attacking each other with such ferocity before. He sank back into the chair and closed his eyes. He didn't want to see anything like that, not today.

It was just after midday when he finally managed to climb out of the recliner. He'd allowed the morning to wash over him in a peaceful daydream and not once had Natalie entered his mind. It had been a beautiful melancholy peace and he'd come to the conclusion that it would be pointless to spend any time in trying to explain it.

He walked into the kitchen and opened the cupboards. There were plenty of tins and of course Ina's cake but not an awful lot else.

"Steak, I fancy a steak."

He felt saliva gather in his mouth. He'd neglected to eat breakfast in his stupor and he was starving. He'd have to drive into town but that was okay. He could visit the supermarket as well as the butcher and get some chips to go with the steak. He looked at the oven. He hadn't cooked anything that couldn't be tipped out of a can so far so he'd definitely need some additional cooking equipment.

He rushed upstairs and grabbed the clothes he'd discarded on the bedroom floor. Today was definitely a steak and chips day, and maybe a bottle of wine too. He dressed quickly and did his best to ignore the bloody bloom on the sheet. If he drove quickly he could be eating rare fillet at a decent hour. He jumped into the car and drove off. Not even the drizzle could lower his mood today, and as for the resurgence of the constant dull ache in his side? Well, when everything else felt this tranquil, that barely mattered, barely mattered at all. Maybe things were looking up, at last.

*

He slapped the steak onto the griddle and took a sip of the wine. He was no connoisseur but it was red, French and on special offer at half price so how bad could it be? The steak sizzled and filled the house with a delicious aroma.

"Cheers." He held his tumbler up. There was no reply but wind whistled through the eaves in approval.

It had been a long time since he'd cooked anything but a couple of minutes on each side was just about as long as he was prepared to wait. He slid it onto the plate and piled some chunky chips beside it. He was almost dribbling as he carried it to the recliner.

As he cut the first butter-soft chunk from the steak, the afternoon finally gave up the ghost and darkness settled outside. Rain lashed at the patio doors and as he tried to look out, his distorted reflection looked back at him.

He pushed the steak into his mouth and felt the bloody juices run down his throat. He emitted a groan of pleasure. The butcher had given him strict instructions about dealing with the lump of meat and he obviously knew a thing or two because it was perfect.

He'd missed a whole day of work but it didn't matter, there were plenty still in the bank, a whole lifetime's worth. Besides, he felt as if he'd made a huge leap forward psychologically and that had to be worth more than a sanded floor or a repaired gutter.

He stuffed more steak into his mouth. Tomorrow he would make a start on the jobs and get them out of the way. He was at Ina's for dinner in the evening and that was the only reason to leave the house. He diverted his gaze from the plate to the window and felt the plate slip from his fingers and fall to the floor.

It wasn't just his own distorted reflection staring back at him.

"I'll slice you open, Stokes. I'll bleed you dry."

Natalie's twisted snarl loomed over his shoulder. The teeth she still had were blackened, broken and sharp. The others were gone, victims of the sweet methadone her body and mind craved. He could feel her festering breath on his neck.

Rain ran down the window making a crazy paving of both the image and his mind.

"You'll never lose me."

She lifted a knife to her lips and kissed it. The blade was covered in blood and as she pulled it away, a clot dangled from her lips. "I'm with you always." She drew the knife along his cheek.

All Stokes could muster was a faint whisper. "You're not there, you're not really there."

"Oh but I am." She trailed the knife in a circle on his cheek and stopped at the corner of his eye.

"I'm in here."

Stokes couldn't move, he couldn't even blink. A tear pooled in his eye and rolled slowly down his cheek.

"You're not there," he repeated, but even to his own ears his voice sounded uncertain.

She licked her cracked lips and flicked her tongue inside his ear.

A faint hiss and she was gone – back to the dark recess in his mind. Stokes wiped the tear from his cheek. He was shivering, not from any chill but in frustrated anger. A few good hours, that was all he'd been allowed. That was all she was prepared to cede.

He flipped over the plate and scooped up the chips. Blood wept from the steak and seeped into the carpet, making a brown stain. He picked up the fork and stabbed it into the meat. There was no way he could eat it now, his appetite had vanished about the same time Natalie had crept up behind him and licked the knife. The steak was going straight into the bin.

"Bitch," he said through gritted teeth.

*

No wistful dreams inhabited his night-time hours. Instead, Stokes sat in the gloom of his bedroom reliving his near-demise. In the scene, Natalie was not the witch who now tormented him but a sad and desperate figure who had been as confused as Stokes himself over what had happened... over what she had done.

Over and over again he felt the knife slide easily through his flesh. Time and time again he saw her standing over him clutching the knife, the evil-looking blade dripping with his blood. And each time he was as powerless to stop it as he had been a year ago.

At some stage he fell asleep. It couldn't have been for very long but when his eyes flicked open the room was light again, albeit it with a dull greyness. He felt utterly lifeless. What a difference twenty-four hours could make.

He was tired but the thought of wallowing in his own depressed thoughts, he knew, was a terrible idea. No, today was a good day for making a start on the carpet. It was a day for filling his mind with sandpaper grades and a sore back.

He dressed quickly, made tea and toast then looked out onto the lake. It was strange but since that first morning when the geese had slaughtered one of their own, he hadn't seen them again. Perhaps they had migrated or just moved on. Whatever the reason he wasn't too worried, he didn't relish the thought of seeing a display like that again.

He turned and looked over at the expanse of garish carpet. It wasn't old but someone had made an expensive and bad choice buying it. Whatever their condition, the floorboards would be a far better option and if they needed a bit of love and affection then so be it.

"A new start, Stokesy, a new start."

*

He walked slowly down the lane toward Ina and Peter's house. He didn't feel like socialising and in truth he was shattered. He'd worked hard all day and three-quarters of the carpet was now removed, along with all of the gripper rods. The carpet was practically new so whoever laid it hadn't stayed around long.

As tired as he was, he recognised that letting Ina down was apt to have far worse consequences than a simple headache brought on by tiredness. In any case, he had a few questions about the history of the cottage and he had a feeling he was about to have dinner with the best people to ask.

He was once again greeted by Peter like a long-lost friend. It was both irritating and warming at the same time. He was shown into a large open-plan room and a glass of warm beer was thrust into his hand. The décor of the room took Stokes by surprise. It was minimalist and modern. The floor was tiled in black and the walls a clean and crisp white. One side of the room was completely glazed and it afforded a stunning panoramic view of the lake.

He looked around for Ina who he assumed must spend most of her time in the kitchen. She wasn't there but steam was rising from one of the pans on the hob.

He sat on one of the two settees that faced the lake. "Beautiful house."

Peter remained standing. "Cost a pretty penny too. All of this is an extension to the original cottage but Ina wanted it and what Ina wants…"

"What's this? Talking about me, are you?"

Stokes stood up and kissed Ina on the cheek. "I was just saying how beautiful your house is. The view is incredible."

"It is, isn't it? This old stick in the mud didn't want it, can you imagine that?"

"It was overpriced, the whole area is. I dare say Jim paid over the odds for his place. You can get twice the size for half the money twenty minutes away."

Stokes nodded. "I know I paid too much but it was worth every penny, if only for the cakes." He smiled at Ina.

"Not every newcomer gets cakes you know."

"Just the pathetic ones eh?"

"Exactly." Ina turned and walked to the kitchen. "I hope you're hungry."

And he was, he was famished. He was pleased he'd made the effort, his mood was better already.

*

"So how long have you two been here?" Stokes scraped his spoon around the bowl, he didn't want to miss a single drop of custard.

Peter's reply surprised him. "Coming up to five years now."

"Is that all? I thought you'd been here much longer."

"Oh? Why's that?"

"You just seem to be... I don't know, part of the furniture, and I don't mean to be rude by that, but it feels like you're at the centre of the village."

Ina stood up. "Looks like you enjoyed that, the pattern's been scraped clean off the bowl."

"Delicious," Stokes grinned.

"I suppose we are but we've always been like that, wherever we've lived. I suppose you could say we're social animals." She took the bowls over to the kitchen. "Coffee?"

"Only if I can help you clean up."

"You most certainly will not. Peter will do that later. We'll have coffee over by the window."

Peter leaned over. "For God's sake don't argue with her, it won't do any good."

"Well it was absolutely beautiful, thank you." Whether

it was the wine or tiredness he didn't know but Stokes felt genuinely fond of both of them. "You've been really kind and you probably don't realise how much that means to me."

Ina and Peter sat on one sofa and Stokes took the other.

"Perhaps we do." Ina smiled at him. "What brings you here, Jim? We know you were a police officer, the estate agent told us that much, and you're not old enough to be retired, at least not in the conventional sense. So what brings you to Stormark?"

"Ah now there's a tale." He didn't want to go into the whole story. For one, they didn't need to know and secondly, he'd thought about it enough over the last twenty-four hours. Tonight was supposed to be Natalie-free.

"The estate agent was correct and yes I am retired. Stormark is a new start for me in lots of ways."

"Medical?" Peter asked.

"My retirement?"

Peter nodded.

"Yep." He changed the subject quickly. "So tell me about the cottage, who lived there before me? I've been coming up here for a while and it's been empty all that time."

Stokes caught the look that passed between Ina and Peter. It was almost imperceptible but it was there and he'd seen it before. Collusion was a tricky thing to hide.

"We never really got to know him," started Ina. "He

kept himself to himself." She turned to Peter. "I don't think he ever came to one of our little gatherings, did he?"

Peter shrugged. "Don't think so."

"I assume he left in a hurry because the cottage was repossessed," Stokes added.

"Like I said, we didn't really know him but it wouldn't surprise me." Ina stifled a yawn.

"Why's that?" Stokes pushed on despite the signal from Ina.

She stood up. "He just seemed like that, a bit of a fly-by-night. I think that coffee should be ready now. How do you take it?"

"Black please." He was out of practice but the little look between the pair indicated Ina's disinterested tone was an act. It was probably nothing but it made him curious. It would wait for another time though, he'd had a pleasant evening and he didn't want to upset anyone, least of all these two.

"Maybe when I get settled properly you'd like to come and be my first dinner guests? I can't promise anything as good as tonight but I make a mean chilli."

"I've got a light ale that goes perfectly with a bit of spice," Peter almost shouted. It was almost as if he'd been holding his breath.

The rest of the evening passed quickly. Stokes never once allowed his eyes to linger on the great expanse of glass. The night made a mirror of the window and he didn't want to risk seeing an uninvited guest sitting beside or standing behind him.

As he walked back along the lane he realised he'd learned almost nothing about the cottage, or about Ina and Peter. He'd not drunk excessively, not by any means, but he wasn't used to it and telling them about his own life had seemed a perfectly natural thing to do. He'd had enough sense not to spill his guts completely though. He smiled to himself at the metaphor. No, there were some aspects of his life he wanted to keep to himself and Natalie was one such facet.

5

Stokes stood up and pressed his hands into the small of his back. There was just one last strip of carpet to pull up and it couldn't happen soon enough. The carpet was well made and scoring it with his knife had been tough work. The boards underneath looked good though and had clearly been waxed in the recent past. Why anyone would want to cover them up was beyond him but at least they had been protected by the carpet.

He knelt down and winced. It wasn't just his back that was sore – there probably wasn't much skin left on his kneecaps either. He worked his fingers under the side and freed the carpet away from the gripper rods, then he started to pull. It was a strangely satisfying sensation as the final stretch of wood was slowly revealed.

As he reached the patio doors, a beam of weak sunlight flashed through and fell on him. It provided no warmth but it was almost as if the sun had come out, albeit briefly, to celebrate with him. He heaved the carpet and stared with curiosity at what he'd revealed.

A small square hatch had been cut into the floorboards and a metal loop had been sunk into it. He pulled the remainder of the carpet back and hauled it off to one side. What was it? The estate agent hadn't mentioned anything about a cellar, it was something he would have most definitely remembered.

He shuffled forward and lifted the loop with his finger. It was icy cold but it lifted easily without a single squeak of resistance. It was brass and had been crafted for this very purpose and probably at some expense. Stokes frowned and lifted the hatch.

Immediately a vile stench washed over him, pushing him back and away from the hole. The force with which the smell had rushed out was almost as if the odour had been held captive and needed to escape, and quickly. He waited a few seconds and edged forward again. He'd been to enough sudden deaths in his time, some of them ripe with age, to know he'd be better off breathing through his mouth, at least for the time being. This wasn't a human smell though, it was too acrid. He pushed the hatch completely to one side and looked into the hole. There was nothing, nothing except a black hole and the smell was still too strong to risk submerging his head into the darkness.

He stood up and opened the patio doors, allowing the cool late-afternoon air to do battle with the sickening stink. He inhaled deeply and closed his eyes. Although the pine trees on the far side of the lake would never show signs that autumn was on the way, the smell of the less-fortunate deciduous trees still swirled about in the wind. It was a delicious smell and one he'd always found comforting. It wouldn't be long until he was forced to try and light the wood burner. He hadn't lit a fire for some time so it might be interesting.

He turned back and looked down at the hole. Now, where had he put the torch?

*

Peter Gauchment looked at his wife. She was cooking or baking something as usual and her apron strings cut deeply into the fat across her broad back. He'd bought the novelty apron for her as a Christmas present two years ago and on the front was a sexy red polka-dot bikini. It had been a long time since she'd actually worn anything quite as revealing as that. Had she ever? He couldn't remember but he didn't relish the idea of seeing her wear one, a real one anyway. He rubbed his chin and sighed.

"Anything the matter?" she called over her shoulder.

"Nothing, just had enough reading for one day. I think I might take a walk."

"Want me to come?"

God no. "I'd rather you finish those cookies, they smell incredible." It was a wonder he wasn't as big as a barn door and it was no surprise she was almost as big as one.

"Don't be too long, it'll be getting dark in an hour or so."

He grabbed his coat from the back of the door. "I

won't be." He heard her speaking to him as he closed the door. It was probably something about keeping warm and not getting his boots wet in the lake. He sighed again, she couldn't just let him go without saying something else, could she? No, there always had to be one last thing, one last inane comment just so she could have the last word.

He looked back at the house and started walking. As beautiful as Stormark was, he didn't intend to go anywhere near the lake today. Nope, today he was walking along the road, back toward a house with a new owner.

*

Stokes shone the little torch into the hole. The stench had subsided a bit but not enough to risk sticking his head all the way in. The beam of light arrowed into the darkness, collecting dust motes and small flying insects as it went. Unfortunately it wasn't strong enough to penetrate into the farthest reaches and he could see precious little. He coughed and waited for an echo but none came back. The space, however large it was, appeared to be dead.

He bit his lip. Should he go in and have a better look? He didn't particularly relish the idea, it looked like the sort of place spiders liked and he wasn't their biggest fan. Besides, he couldn't see where the floor was. What he really needed was a decent torch to light it up properly, a torch like the one he'd used when he was a copper. It had gone the way of the rest of his kit though – into the bin at the station on his last day. That torch had been everywhere with…

A scratching sound came from the hole. It was distant at first and then it grew louder and louder until it was beneath him, right beneath the hatch. He shone the torch directly down and peered a little closer. The sound stopped immediately.

Two little amber gems burned like coals in the darkness before vanishing again. The sound of scuttling and scratching grew fainter again.

"Rats," he hissed.

Rats came a close second to spiders in his league table of dislikeable creatures and now that he'd found them living in his house, they were apt to move up a place. The ammonia indicated there was at least one nest down there and God alone knew how many rats that meant.

He grabbed the hatch and slotted it back into place. He couldn't see the bottom of the pit but rats were good climbers, he just hoped they weren't any good at lifting heavy objects. Tonight wasn't the right time to be investigating it and tomorrow he'd have to go back to town and pick up some traps, or was poison the weapon of choice? He pulled his chair over the hatch and walked to the front door. The house needed a good through-draft to clear the stench. Sooner or later he'd have to go down there and put an end to them one way or another. His skin crawled at the thought.

He unlocked the front door and allowed fresh air to come rushing in. It was dusk and the landscape that had been alive just a few minutes before was now becoming a lifeless silhouette. The road was elevated from the house by a couple of metres but he seldom heard any traffic during the day and it was even rarer after dark. It would be a while until he was accustomed to the silence and lack of humans.

He squinted and peered into the half-light. Was that a person standing up there on the road looking down at the cottage?

"Hello?" he called out. The road was not only elevated from the house but it was also a good twenty metres away. With the light fading, it was difficult to see any detail. He edged forward to try and see better but before he'd moved more than a step the figure started walking away, down toward the village.

"Hello?" he called again but his shout went unanswered. Was it one of the villagers? If it was then why hadn't they simply answered him or waved? Presumably he'd met most of them by now so he wasn't a curiosity anymore. Whoever it was had just been standing and looking down at the cottage, at him. He suddenly felt very cold and exposed and went back inside. It was probably just some rambler taking in the view, that was all. He locked and bolted the door behind him.

*

Stokes lay on top of the duvet with his Kindle in his lap. Before he'd left for the wilds of Stormark and a house without broadband, he'd loaded up the device with over a hundred books. Some had been on his wish-list for years and some were just random purchases. He had no idea how long it would take to get through them all and some, in particular the classics, might take a little longer than others.

He flipped through the library and although his genre of choice had always been horror, he hadn't read anything like that in a year. He stopped at the Stephen King collection and paused. You couldn't just stop reading horror stories because your life was more horrifying than anything ever written. That was almost as bad as not facing up to the event itself.

He closed his eyes and pressed the screen. "Surprise me if you can, Mr King."

*

At first the sound was easy to ignore. It was like a gentle rain on the window, tap-tapping in a soft and easy rhythm. Stokes turned over and pulled the quilt around his bare shoulder. The sound would soothe him back to sleep if he allowed it to wash over him, if he didn't open his eyes. But now he needed the toilet and the more he thought about not really wanting the toilet, the more he needed it. Besides, it wasn't really raining outside was it? That sound wasn't really the mellow dance of rain drops on the roof.

It wasn't tapping either. It was scratching, harsh and aggressive scratching. He felt his mind lurch from half-sleep to awake in one leap and he was powerless to stop it. He'd spent enough nights wrestling with his mind's will to know it was futile. If his mind said that two hours of sleep were quite enough, then it was, and there was no point trying to argue. Especially not when it sounded like something was trying to eat the insides out of the cottage.

He rubbed his face and felt the burgeoning beard beneath his fingers. It had been several days since his last shave and his face felt itchy and uncomfortable. He blinked rapidly to bring his eyes into focus and listened.

The noise stopped for a moment and then continued.

Scretch, scretch, scretch. A pause and then, *scretch, scretch, scretch.*

He knew what it was even before he started down the stairs but he went anyway. He instantly regretted not putting his shorts on or a t-shirt at least, the little cottage was icy cold.

He pushed the recliner to the side and stamped on the hatch.

"Shut up down there!"

Rats didn't understand English because the scratching continued. There wasn't much he could do about the racket tonight, he'd just have to pull the duvet a bit tighter around his ears and hope for the best.

Stokes dropped to one knee, he had no intention of lifting the hatch but he wanted to make sure they had all heard him. He lowered his head and spoke to the metal ring. "Make the most of your little party. Tomorrow you'll all be dead."

"So will you," a voice hissed from beneath him.

Stokes staggered backward, away from the hatch. His breath came in short gasps. No, he hadn't heard that, he hadn't heard Natalie's voice.

"No," he whispered and took another step back.

Scretch, scretch, scretch.

But the sound wasn't from the hole in the ground. It was from the window – from the patio window. He didn't want to look up, with all his soul he didn't want to look up. He wanted to stare down at his naked feet for the rest of his life, he wanted to count the wrinkles on each of his toes because if he did that he wouldn't have to face Natalie Sutton ever again.

Scretch, scretch, scretch.

He raised his head and looked at the window. Natalie's disembodied head loomed out of the darkness and pressed against the glass. Her face was hideously distorted as she pressed it harder and harder against the glass, harder and harder until she threatened to push through.

Stokes breath came in ragged gasps. "How long are you going to torment me?" his voice cracked.

"As long as it takes," she hissed back and ran her tongue along the glass, leaving a dark smear.

"You're mine," she laughed and was gone.

Stokes wiped his mouth with the back of his shaking hand. How long was this going to go on for? How long before he couldn't cope anymore? Before the little cracks in his mind turned into a fragile crazy paving and he fell right through to... to where?

He looked down at his feet. He wasn't sure but Natalie was winning. It didn't matter if he moved to the other side of the world, it didn't matter if he moved to the moon, she would always be there. She would always be a part of him, a dirty, sordid and violent part of him and he would never escape. She wouldn't let him.

He dropped to his knees and then rolled onto his side. The bare boards were cold against his naked flesh but he didn't care.

Scretch, scretch, scretch.

The rats had no interest in him or his ghosts, they just wanted to bite.

6

Stokes peeled his face up off the floorboards. A mixture of sawdust and spittle had dried in the corner of his mouth and it tasted terrible. He'd woken up with worse hangovers but his body felt in a similar condition. He shivered involuntarily and stood up. At some point last night he must have fallen asleep. Was it sleep, or was it his mind shutting down completely?

Like before.

He wasn't going down that road today or any other day, once was enough. This had been sleep, plain old sleep, and Natalie's deformed face pressing against the glass was just another hallucination. He walked to the doors and looked out. Morning had broken but not that long ago, and a thin mist tried its best to cling to the lake's surface. He looked at his wrist but his watch was lying on the floor beside the bed.

The rats must have slept too because he didn't remember being disturbed by them again but... What if he had shut down again? What if his brain had decided that it was safer just to flick the switch than to try to process another nightmare? He opened the door to let some of the rats' stink out and felt the cold air caress his naked crotch with cold and spiky fingers.

The doctor said he was suffering from post-traumatic stress. No shit, Sherlock. And that the brain often came up with its own solutions for keeping someone alive in high stress situations. That was right after he'd written a prescription for some heavy-duty tranquillisers. The doctor clearly didn't trust Stokes's body to shut down at the right time.

He hadn't shut down when Natalie stabbed him though, and things didn't get much more stressful than that. Oh no, dear old brain had given him the pleasure of feeling each and every millimetre of steel as it was driven into his body. Stokes pushed his own face against the glass.

"Bitch."

He turned around and looked at the hatch. "And you lot can get ready." Today was not going to be one of those days. Today was not going to be a day of regret, reproach and bitterness. Today was going to be a day of action and of extermination.

"New start, Stokesy, new start."

*

Stokes was at the hardware shop before it opened but he didn't care. He sat in the car and ate breakfast while he waited. There was a McDonald's restaurant just across the road and something a bit greasy fitted the bill perfectly. One day he'd have to register at the doctors, but then there would be the pre-registry health check and the history run-down.

"And how do you feel now, Mr Stokes?"

"Just fine and dandy, thanks. Now if you can carve Natalie's nasty little face right out of my mind, I'll be on my way."

He swallowed the last mouthful of muffin and sipped the scalding tea. Two workers let themselves into the shop and disappeared inside, laughing.

"What's the worst you have to contend with, then? A cold and uncaring wife? A slow day on lawnmower sales? Try seeing the ghost of the woman who tried to kill you each and every day, then we'll see how much you're laughing."

He tipped the rest of the tea out of the window and dropped the cup in the passenger foot-well. It was exactly eight o'clock and the shop should be open. He wiped his mouth on the paper napkin and tossed it beside the cup.

"I want rat poison and I want a lot of it." He climbed out of the car and walked across the deserted car park.

These places were the same in every town and city across the country. They smelled the same, they sold the same things and they all piped the same headache-inducing music. He walked impatiently up and down the aisles until he finally found what he was looking for... at least he thought he had. The music was starting to really irritate him, even more so because he'd started to hum along.

"Stop it," he whispered to himself.

The selection of poisons and traps was astounding and at the same time utterly confusing. He stared at the boxes, lifting them off the shelf randomly. What he really needed was a big box with 'I kill rats' and a red X on the front. But that wasn't the case, the word 'humane' seemed to feature heavily on all the packaging. For Stokes that came down the list and several places behind 'extermination'.

"Can I help you, sir?"

Stokes turned and was faced by a grinning adolescent.

"Err… what do you know about rats?"

The youth smiled back. "Quite a lot actually. I have several as pets."

"Oh." Stokes looked at the assistant's name badge. His name was Danny and beneath his name were the words Just ask!

"I'm looking for poison or traps, or both. Anything that can get rid of them really."

Danny looked horrified. "Get rid of them? Do you need to, I mean do you really need to? Most people don't understand them, they're actually clean ani…"

Stokes held up his hand. "Look, I know you mean well but I'm not a fan and I'd just like some advice, please."

Danny looked at him as if he'd just crapped on the shop floor. "I really couldn't tell you which is the best, they all do the same thing, kill animals."

Stokes heard a trace of something in Danny's voice, something disapproving.

"How old are you, Danny?"

"Twenty-two but I don't see…"

"A bit of advice for you, when someone asks for something in your shop, don't give them your opinion, just help them."

Danny turned and walked away but this time Stokes definitely heard something, he heard *a tut*. A rage erupted from nowhere.

"Did you just tut at me?"

The youth turned around and looked at him. His expression was a barely disguised sneer. "No."

Stokes took a step toward him. "Yes you did, I heard you tut."

Danny stayed exactly where he was. "No, you misheard." His tone was one of defiance.

Stokes took another step forward. You tutted at me, you little shit. It had been a while but he knew what adrenalin felt like when it slipped silently into his bloodstream.

"I don't think so." He drew his lips back across his teeth.

Danny stepped back. Stokes felt a brief wave of pleasure as fear flashed across the other man's face.

"Sorry, I didn't mean anything by it. I just… I just…"

"But you tutted." Stokes was now just a foot away from Danny. Who the hell did this little shit think he was? Judging him like that. "Now you'll apologise to me." Stokes clenched his fists. If the kid wanted to get clever with him then he might have to teach him some manners.

"Apologise," Stokes demanded. There wouldn't be another request. He closed the gap and they were now face to face. *Are you ready for this, Danny? I've had one hell of a year and I'm ready to pop. You just might have the lucky ticket for some special audience participation…*

"Sorry, I'm sorry." Danny backed away two or three steps then turned heel and ran down the aisle.

Stokes watched and his grimace was replaced by a smile. That'll teach him. He stood there for a moment and then as his fists unclenched, he cringed. Oh God, that wasn't right. That wasn't Jim Stokes. Why had he behaved like that? It was like an animal.

He snatched an armful of items from the shelf and piled them into the basket. He just wanted to get out of there.

He paid and almost ran across the car park. What he'd done was utterly shameful and there was no excuse for it. He did everything but smack the kid across the face. He threw everything onto the back seat and then just sat in the car. It was wrong, all very wrong. He should go back and apologise to Danny. Tell him he was sorry and that he was… what? Tired? Stressed? What exactly? Telling someone that every day you still saw the face of the woman who'd stabbed you wasn't a good idea. It was apt to land you in hospital. So what would you tell him? Would you tell him you were scared? Is that what you'd say? Just march right on in there and tell him, *'Listen, Danny, I'm sorry but I'm scared to death. I'm scared that this bitch I see each and every day only did half a job when she tried to gut me. She's finishing the job now but this time she's in my head poking about. Oh and by the way, she's still got her nasty little blade with her and she's taking ragged little chunks out of my brain. She's a real stunner too. How would you like to meet her? Sure I can't tempt you, Danny boy?'*

Stokes turned the ignition and revved the engine. He was tense and his right foot had a burning desire to see exactly how fast he could take the B-road back to Stormark. He couldn't put his hands around Natalie's throat and choke her but he could kill some rats. He could completely annihilate them. He put the car into first and drove out of the still-deserted car park.

"Sorry, Danny."

*

He should have bought a better torch, and if *Just ask!* Danny hadn't been so eager to display his feelings about the killing of rats then he would have. He stared into the hole and bit his lip.

"They're only rats, Stokesy. Man up."

He looked at his purchases and picked up two packets with 'Rat Killer Box' on the front. According to the packaging, there was no need to handle any poison and each one could kill ten rats. He didn't know how many were down there but this was a good start. He looked at the hole again and then at the boxes.

"It's time."

The hatch was just about wide enough to accommodate him but it was a snug fit. He gripped the torch beneath his teeth and lowered himself down. It couldn't be too deep, the rat's eyes had been clear and bright. Just as his shoulders started to complain about supporting him, the tips of his toes touched solid ground. He rested his chin on the dusty floorboards as he gathered some extra inner steel to drop into the hole completely.

Had something just run over his foot?

He closed his eyes and grimaced. Even if it had, so what? What was it going to do?

"Nothing," he answered his own question.

He released his elbows and shoulders from the edge of the hatch and dropped down. Almost instantly he shone the torchlight down at his toes. There were no traces of any vermin and beneath his trainers was what looked like soil. He shone the weak torchlight around. If he wanted to move around in there, he'd have to do it hunched over in an awkward position. He reached up and grabbed the boxes. He had no intention on moving around any more than was absolutely necessary but there was no point in putting the boxes right next to each other.

He placed the first one next to his feet. The soil was a fine powder and as dry as a bone. He shuddered, it probably wasn't just soil but years of rat crap he'd just touched. The stench wasn't as bad as the previous day but it was still strong and he covered his nose with the palm of his hand. He shuffled forward, crouching under the supporting beams. It was dark down here and although the house was well above the water line, he wondered if there was a chance of flooding in heavy rain. He flicked the light toward the direction of the lake but he could see nothing except unending darkness. He doubted even a powerful Maglite could reach into the gloom. This was a cavernous space and two traps wasn't going to be enough, not by a long chalk.

He dropped down, carefully avoiding putting his knee in the dirt, and placed the other trap down. A scratching noise came from behind him and he nearly smashed his head into the beams above in his haste to spin around. If there was a bleaker place on this earth, he'd yet to see it.

"Enough," he muttered and staggered back toward the hatch. One day, that was all he'd give it, then he'd come back with the rest of his arsenal and try something else. Once that lot ran out, he might have to find a new shop if he needed anything else. He doubted Danny would be waiting with open arms to welcome him back.

*

Stokes pulled the recliner back over the hatch and sat on it. He had a bottle of beer in one hand and his torch in the other. He hadn't heard anything from them all day but he already knew they liked to come out at night. For animals that obviously preferred to exist in the perpetual gloom of a hole, they certainly knew how to hold a party once the lights upstairs went out.

He sipped his beer. It was the last bottle of Peter's brew and it tasted good. Dusk had settled over the lake and with it came a slight sense of dread. Natalie had by no means been exclusively nocturnal in her appearances but she'd certainly seemed to enjoy that time of day, especially since they'd both moved out to Stormark.

Would he go to bed? Was it worth it? He dropped the torch on the floor and wriggled out of the chair. A night spent on the cold floorboards had made his body ache in all the wrong places. A night spent on the recliner was apt to render him immobile for a week. One thing was for absolute certain and that was his weariness. And if weariness was a problem now, how bad would it be in a week from now? Things couldn't continue like this for much longer, they just couldn't.

He undressed, dropping his clothes in an untidy pile beside the bed, and slid under the duvet. He closed his eyes and saw his hands around Danny's scrawny neck. He was simply too tired to prevent his mind from playing the whole fantasy out.

*

Scretch, scretch, screeetch.

Stokes pushed the pillow against his ears. Not again. How long had he been asleep? It didn't feel like long.

Scretch, scretch, scretch.

The noise echoed around the cottage as if it were an underground cavern. If he got up and banged on the hatch, would it shut them up? And if it did, then for how long?

Scretch, scretch, scretch.

And if he got up and went downstairs, what horrors would his mind conjure up from the shadows? He lay still waiting for the next bout but there was only the sound of wind weaving through the trees and slithering around the eaves of the cottage. It was at once comforting and disturbing. He felt himself drifting back to the point of sleep.

Scretch, scretch, screeeetch.

"Enough," he barked into the gloom and jumped out of bed. How dare that bitch stab him? How dare that fucking bitch carry on stabbing him, each and every day?

He leapt down the stairs and went straight to the kitchen. He knew what he wanted and where it was, but the moon guided him perfectly and shone a spotlight of silver light onto the knife block. He touched the handle of the cruel-looking paring knife and felt the icy-cold steel send a pleasant shock through his flesh.

"Is this a dagger which I see before me?"

He turned toward the hatch and smiled. The moonlight bounced off the blade but the reflection was nowhere near as bright as that from off his bared teeth.

He took two steps toward the hatch, pausing only to reach down for the torch, and shoved the recliner back from the hole with his bare foot. Danny would be pretty upset to see what was about to happen. It was about to get messy, messy and as far away from humane as it was possible to be.

He pulled open the hatch and dropped the lit torch into the pit.

"I know I'm not invited but I'm coming anyway." He didn't notice the cool, ammonia-laced air rise up and tickle the hair on his balls. He had one thing on his mind, slitting as many throats as he could find.

Scretch, scretch, scretch.

He dropped down and lowered himself into the hole.

The soil, or detritus, or whatever it was, felt surprisingly warm beneath his toes. It was almost like walking on a beach, not that he could really remember how that felt, it had been so long. He was angry. No, he didn't feel angry, he'd gone way past that. He felt clarity. The kind of certainty which comes when you've set your mind on a course of action and you know it's within your grasp to make it happen.

"Here, ratty, ratty, ratty." He made a squeaking noise and laughed at himself. No doubt they'd run away to all corners by now and buried themselves in the festering cesspits they called home. He looked down at the trap but he wasn't expecting to see anything in it. He wasn't disappointed.

"Oh, don't be like that. Come out and play."

He crouched as still as he could and waited for the slightest indication of where they were. It felt good to be holding the knife, he felt powerful. Above him a floorboard creaked but he barely noticed as he waited, eyes searching the darkness for gems of amber light glistening in the murk.

"Come out, come out wherever you are," he hissed. He could feel himself losing patience. He edged farther away from the hatch and from the torch. This was their territory but they couldn't hide from him, not a chance. He peered into the darkness and waited again. Sooner or later one of them would come out again. Sooner or later they would have to start gnawing on whatever it was they were so fond of chewing.

"Where are you?" he called.

"I'm here," a voice whispered into his ear.

Stokes swallowed hard, forcing the bile back down his throat.

"I'm behind you, Stokes." He didn't need to turn around to know who it was.

"And I'm ready for you, bitch." He turned quickly and swung the knife as he did. His head told him it was a stupid, futile gesture but it made him feel better.

The blade swept cleanly through her face, carving a neat line across her features. He grinned and thrust the knife into her left eye socket before slashing the blade across her face again.

"It hurts doesn't it!" he roared and carried on trying to hack her to pieces. In the background, in the part of his brain which clung to reason, he was screaming at himself. Screaming at his own stupidity. This was not a real person, this was nothing more than a vision conjured up by his damaged mind; a toy with which to torture him. Yet he slashed, cut and drove the knife into the only thing he could find – the ghost of a woman who had tried to end his life and had succeeded with her own.

Soon nothing was left and Stokes dropped to his knees in the dirt. What was he doing here? What was he doing, crawling around in the dirt like a rat?

"I'm behind you," her voice whispered again.

He clutched the knife tightly and rose to his feet. He felt very cold all of a sudden and his arms ached but he wanted to fight on – he needed to.

"Just shut up!" he screamed.

Natalie laughed and caught the blade between her rotten teeth. He pulled the blade back and raised it above his head.

"I said shut up!" He drove the blade down through her matted hair and into her skull.

She made a noise like air being squeezed from a balloon, but her stupid grin showed the same old drug-induced defiance. He slashed and cut and stabbed and thrust but with each attack she only laughed back at him.

He dropped to his knees and wiped his hands over his body. His skin was covered in a cold sweat and he wasn't sure if he could lift the blade again. *It's just an image created by your sick mind, nothing more.* His inner voice was faint but had it been as loud as a siren, he would not have listened.

"Help me, someone please help me." Even in the darkness his fingers found the scar on his torso. His fingers would always be able to find that.

Natalie loomed over him again and he looked up. "What do you want from me?"

She simply smiled down at him. Rats tumbled from her hair and scuttled off squealing into the shadows.

"You want another pound of flesh, is that it?" He traced his greasy fingers over the scar again.

"But that's not enough is it, Natalie? You want it all,

don't you? You want me to suffer."

He drew the knife over the scar and felt the flesh pucker beneath the blade.

She licked her lips.

He flicked the blade and winced as it picked at the scar tissue.

"Is that good?" he asked.

He pushed the knife a little harder and gasped as the tip of the blade slipped beneath the surface of his skin.

"More? You want more?" he snarled.

Natalie's eyes settled on his and for a moment they were locked together. Stokes frowned. Was she crying in there? Beneath the lunatic scrutiny of this mirage, was Natalie Sutton actually weeping?

He pulled the submerged tip of the blade across the length of the scar, opening it up entirely. He screamed out in agony and dropped the sticky knife into the dirt.

"You were crying. The day you stabbed me, you were crying." He covered the wound with his hand and felt the warmth of the blood seep through his fingers.

"I was trying to help you." He reached out to touch Natalie's face. "Help me?"

A cold breath on his shoulder made him flinch.

"I will help you. Stay with me." It was not Natalie's tone which fell on his ears but the voice of another and he recognised it. It was the voice of the dream who had come to him just two nights before.

"Help me," he whispered and fell face first into the dirt.

*

Edward Willis felt his eyes bulging in their sockets as Stokes rushed past him. Had he seen him? He held his breath for an eternity as Stokes rummaged around in the kitchen for something. He couldn't move, not even if Lucifer himself was poking him up the backside with a burning spike. What on earth was he doing in there? Cooking dinner? It was a little late to be up to those sort of tricks. And what was he mumbling about? He covered the face of his watch to shield the fluorescent face. Besides, when he'd left home it had been just after three which meant it couldn't be much later than half past by now.

This had been an impromptu decision, made in the early hours. In the silence of his bedroom, at a time known only to the stressed, guilty and the insomniacs. He'd listened to the owl screeching its way toward dawn and thrown back the covers in bad-tempered haste. He didn't need to look for the key, it was where it had been for the past two years – buried deep inside his sock drawer.

He flinched as Stokes reappeared. Christ, the man was clutching a knife and he was utterly naked. Their eyes locked for an eternity. This had been a mistake, a huge and silly mistake. He opened his mouth to speak, to apologise for this terrible error of judgement but before he could, Stokes looked away.

The man looked deranged. God alone knew what he was planning to do with the knife but it wasn't cooking. He watched as Stokes pushed the chair away with his foot and revealed the hatch. The moonlight bounced off the blade and illuminated the brass loop.

Willis swallowed and felt nauseous. He could vomit at any moment, he was absolutely sure of that. What on earth was this lunatic doing? He couldn't be thinking about going down there, surely not. But he watched as Stokes lifted the hatch and shouted something down into the darkness. He couldn't hear what it was because Stokes's words sounded garbled. Then the man simply leapt into the hole, clutching the knife.

He took a step forward. This wasn't good. This wasn't good at all.

7

"Good to see you again, Jim." Peter pumped his hand with the usual enthusiasm.

Stokes smiled and nodded.

"You okay? You don't look very well."

Stokes didn't feel very well, in fact he felt terrible. "Fine, just got a bit of a cold coming I think."

It had been three days since he'd been in the pit with Natalie and he remembered it all, every last thrust of his knife, every last scream of pain and anguish. His body remembered it too. The aching arms, the stiff neck and the wound on his torso which throbbed with every thumping beat of his heart.

"Sorry to hear that. Come on, I've got something to help bring you back to life."

Stokes allowed himself to be dragged across the room. He didn't have the energy to resist. This all felt so false, so pathetic and pointless, yet why had he come? Why on earth had he come to this wretched little meeting?

Peter pushed a glass into his hand. "Here, drink this and tell me what you think."

Stokes was aware of the chatter behind him, it was almost deafening. "I'm not sure I c…"

"Come on, don't be a killjoy. I brewed it up especially for tonight."

Stokes tipped the glass back and swallowed. "It's good, Peter, very good." A cold sweat had broken out on his forehead and he wiped it with the back of his hand.

"I knew you'd like it! Come on, drink up, there's plenty more where that came from."

Stokes looked at the empty seats behind him. "I think I'll just go and sit down for a minute."

"Of course, just come and get another pint when you're ready."

He walked over to the side of the room and sat down. A middle-aged couple smiled at him and he smiled back, holding up his glass to them. What were their names? Bill and Lois? He wiped his head again. It didn't matter anyway.

"Cheers." He raised his glass for the second time.

He knew why he'd come tonight. He needed to know he wasn't dead. He needed to see other humans and engage with them. He needed to feel the warmth of their breath on his face and to hear their voices. But even now he couldn't be sure.

He could remember everything except how he got back to his bed. For three days he had lain there, staring out of the roof window. Time had passed, was passing, while he lay there but it was abstract and meaningless. It was pointless.

"Oh, Peter was right, you look terrible, Jim."

Stokes looked up. "I'm fine honestly, Ina. It's just a bout of man-flu, that's all."

"Hmm well you look like you need an early night to me. Where is she?"

He swallowed hard and tried to look calm. How did Ina know about Natalie? His mind hadn't created the Natalie illusion since he'd slashed her to bits in the pit but how did she know?

"She?"

"Yes, this girl who's been keeping you up all night. You call it man-flu, I call it love's young dream. You haven't slept for days by the looks of you." She winked at him.

He would've laughed but he knew it would sound like a cackle. He smiled and shook his head instead. "Just the man-flu, Ina, just the man-flu."

"I'm keeping my eye on you, Mr Stokes." She marched off.

That felt a bit better now. Just that little exchange had brought him back from the brink of whatever new abyss he now found himself teetering on.

He turned to the couple beside him. "I'm really sorry, I don't remember your names." Genial conversation with a couple of pensioners was what he needed right now and these two fit the bill perfectly.

"I'm Bill and this is my wife Louise."

Stokes nodded. So close.

*

He pulled the collar up on his jacket but it did little to protect his neck. He'd have to dust off the old duffel coat soon, if he could find it. He felt a little better than he had when he first arrived at the gathering, more alive anyway. Whether that was Peter's brew or the normality of the event was up for debate, but it was a welcome feeling. How would he feel when he got back to the cottage? There was only one way to find out.

"New start, Stokesy, new start." He'd repeated that mantra almost every day during the last six months and how many times had he believed it? He shivered and started walking back up the hill. Was that snow in the air? He stuck out his tongue and tilted his head back. The estate agent had told him the roads were more or less impassable once the snow started but surely this was too early? He shivered again. The seasons were all messed up nowadays anyway. If it was cold enough to snow, it was cold enough, whether it was late autumn or mid-summer.

He ambled along the road, keeping his neck tucked down into his ineffective collar. What would he find when he got back? Would Natalie be waiting for him again? He licked his lips. Less than two minutes away from the gathering and already he was starting to feel ill again.

He stopped and looked up. The cottage was less than five minutes away and he could just about see the chimney above the brow of the hill. He should sell it. He should just get rid of it and never step foot inside it again. Already it held too many memories and most of them bad. How long could he keep running though? He'd faced her and destroyed her over and over again with the knife, yet she'd won. Somehow she'd won because he was standing here thinking about selling the house, selling his new start after it had barely begun. He resumed walking. He didn't have the energy to move house again, not yet at least.

His stomach turned in a nauseating whirl. Someone was standing on the brow of the hill. Again, it was just a silhouette but whoever it was appeared to be staring down at him.

"Hello?" Stokes shouted and quickened his pace.

The figure made no move until he shouted for the second time, then they dropped down the other side of the rise and disappeared. Stokes broke into a jog. His days of being able to sprint were gone but he knew he could last at a steady pace until he reached the cottage.

He reached the top of the hill and paused. He might as well have been staring down into the pit beneath the floorboards. He'd left the lights on inside and they threw down small squares of illumination onto the land directly beside the cottage. Other than that, there was no sign of life at all.

"Hello?" he shouted again and waited.

When no reply came, he started walking. Everything felt very close to the edge and if he stopped and waited for too long he was liable to fall off.

He put the key into the lock and turned it. The door clicked open and he waited. He waited for Natalie to come rushing and gouge his eyeballs out with her fingernails. But something felt different. Was it the smell? No, there were still the traces of ammonia and single man in the air, so what was it?

He took a step inside and locked the door. It wasn't a smell and it wasn't even something he could see, it was a feeling, that was all. He looked over at the hatch. It wasn't pushed down properly and one corner was raised above the other floorboards. He walked over and kicked at it, knocking it into place like an errant piece of jigsaw puzzle.

He'd lost his mind down there, there was no arguing about that. If it wasn't for his pain threshold, he might have gutted himself too. He wriggled out of his jacket and lifted his shirt. Earlier on he'd taped a tea-towel to his skin in the absence of anything closely resembling a first aid kit. It was crude but at least it covered the wound. He peeled it back and winced. Jagged bits of flesh on the edge of the wound tried desperately to cling to the fibres of the towel. A faint sour whiff drifted up to his nose. He should probably go to the doctors and have it checked out. He'd just tell them he caught it when he was doing repairs to the house. He pushed the towel back over the wound and walked upstairs. He removed his clothing as he went and left it where it fell. All that walking had made him hot, very very hot and tired.

He flopped into the bed and started to drift off to sleep. He felt surprisingly relaxed now he was back. Natalie could come and disembowel him for all he cared.

Scretch, scretch, scretch.

Stokes stirred and climbed under the duvet. He was cold but too tired to do anything except find a comfortable sleeping position.

He was too tired to open his eyes and see the figure standing at the bottom of his bed, watching him sleep. He didn't even stir when the little girl opened her mouth and allowed a starving and filthy rat to scurry from between her teeth. If he had awoken and seen her, or the rat, he would have assumed he was having a very bad dream. He murmured in his sleep. The little girl smiled and ground the stumps of her blackened teeth together. *Scretch scretch scretch.*

*

Stokes clung to the rim of the toilet and vomited. Each shuddering heave made him cry out in pain as his wound opened and closed. There was little more than a bright yellow bile coming up now but that wasn't surprising since he couldn't remember eating anything for several days. This was the worse bout of man-flu he'd ever had.

He wiped his mouth and stood up. His face looked drawn and grey in the mirror, just like a heroin addict. He turned the cold tap on and filled his mouth with icy water. One day he'd look back on this and laugh, like a lunatic perhaps, but he'd laugh all the same.

He'd slept like a log last night and by his reckoning had nearly twelve hours of solid, unbroken rest. So why did he feel so dog-tired? He spat the water into the sink and filled his mouth a second time. He swallowed it and immediately brought it back up again.

He should just go downstairs and sit in the recliner for a while. Looking out at the lake had to be better than staring at his own ugly reflection. He grabbed his duvet and took the stairs at the only pace he could manage – snail's. When he reached the last step, he paused as another wave of nausea gripped him. He took several deep breaths and padded across the room, feeling each and every freezing inch of floorboard beneath his feet. If he ever got round to it, he'd have to hoover up all the dust he'd made.

He stopped beside the hatch and felt the room rotate around him like some sickening fairground ride. He was glued to the spot.

"She is gone," he whispered.

The letters were crude and child-like but they were there, scratched into the layers of dust which covered the hatch.

"She is gone?" he repeated and dropped to his knees. What was this? He looked about the room for signs that someone was inside.

"Who did this?" he shouted.

He looked down at the words and traced his finger along the letters. The wood was cold beneath his fingers. "She… is… gone," he said each word as he finished it.

Had he written it himself? A bead of sweat dripped off his forehead and made a splash mark in the dust. It smudged some of the letters, rendering it unreadable. He stared at it for a moment before wiping his hands over the whole lot.

"Now you're gone." He got to his feet and groaned. His body ached all over, including his head. What he really needed was a good measure of whisky and a dozen painkillers to knock him out. He looked over at the kitchen and turned away. There was no use looking over there for help. There wasn't much in there besides a few packets of dried noodles and some tins of beans. He slumped into the chair and pulled the duvet tightly around him. Strange writing in the dust was pretty low down on the scale of weirdness at the moment. He'd just have to put it on the shelf for now, right below the photograph of dear Natalie.

He threw his head back and laughed. "Oh Natalie, Natalie! Wherefore art thou, Natalie?"

He retched and dribbled yellow bile onto the duvet.

Without a doubt, this was the worst man-flu ever.

And why wouldn't the rats stop scratching? It was daylight and they were at it again.

Scretch, scretch, scretch.

It sounded like they were in the room with him now. They probably were but there wasn't anything he could do about it.

Scretch, scretch, scretch.

Not only in the room but in his head too.

8

Darkness. Complete and utter darkness. So dark that she could barely see her hands until they touched her nose.

She screamed. And then she screamed again and she didn't stop until her throat felt as if it was full of thistles. Then she retched, a terrible and dry heave which left her gasping for breath.

Where was she?

She shivered and pulled her knees up to her chest. The mattress was thin and she could feel the cold, damp earth creeping through its fibres. She shouldn't have just her nightie on, not when it was this cold.

Was there a blanket on the mattress? She fumbled around until she felt the itchy, scratchy rug they used to lay out on the grass for picnics.

Where was she?

It smelled funny here too. It smelled a bit like the house after Mummy had done a spring clean. Except it wasn't a clean smell, it was dirty and it hurt her nose to breathe.

Was it a dream?

It must be because… well… because it was so dark and nowhere was as dark as this except in a dream.

In a nightmare.

She screamed again but her throat felt like it did when she had to see the doctor that time. That was the time the doctor with the funny eye had given her some horrible medicine that tasted like bananas. She hated bananas too but she'd taken it because he'd said it would make her feel better. Mummy and Daddy said he was a nice man and a good doctor but he wasn't. He wasn't nice at all. He'd looked at her funny. He'd given her a bad feeling.

"Mummy? Daddy?" she called out.

She'd read somewhere that pinching yourself when you were dreaming made you wake up right away. She pinched the skin on her wrist and closed her eyes.

"One… two… three," she whispered and opened her eyes.

How could she still be dreaming? She obviously wasn't doing it right.

She pinched the skin on her cheek hard enough to make tears come. "One… two… three…"

What if it wasn't a dream? What if one of those nasty men that Mummy sometimes talked about had come and taken her?

"Mummy?"

No, that couldn't have happened. Daddy would have bashed them with his hammer if one of those sort of men had come to the house. Mummy and Daddy loved her. They wouldn't let anything happen to her. They'd be looking for her by now too, so would the policemen.

She started to cry. What if the policemen couldn't find her? What if Mummy and Daddy couldn't find her either and the nasty man did something nasty to her?

What exactly was *something nasty* anyway? Nobody ever said exactly what that was. How did you know who the nasty men were? And how many of them were there? There could be hundreds for all she knew.

Some men, like Doctor Wilde, gave her a bad feeling but that didn't make them nasty men. She knew that because sometimes Daddy gave her a bad feeling too. Only a little one though and it was only when he didn't know she was watching and he was alone with Mummy. She didn't like it though, it made her tummy feel funny.

Sometimes though there were pictures too. Like the time she walked to the park holding Mummy's hand and a group of boys bumped into them. One of the boys had horrible, frightening pictures in his brain. She'd screamed then, she couldn't help herself. And then she'd pointed at him and tried to explain to Mummy what she'd seen. But the words wouldn't come out properly. Or had she been too little to know enough of the right words?

It had frightened Mummy though and she'd told her off. And then when they were back home again, Mummy had hugged her and said she was sorry for shouting. That was before she did the really bad things.

"Mummy?"

She wished Mummy was here right now to give her a cuddle. It seemed that right now nearly everyone gave her a bad feeling.

"Daddy!"

She curled up in a ball and closed her eyes. If she went back to sleep then everything would be better when she woke up again. She might have toast for breakfast in the morning, toast and raspberry jam.

*

When she woke up she was cold, very, very cold and the lights were still off. Maybe she hadn't slept that long and it wasn't quite morning yet? It was always dark when she woke up on Christmas morning, but that was always very early.

What was that scratching noise? It sounded a bit like when Daddy ran his fingers across his beard. Never mind, it was probably just a crow in the garden. The smell was still the same as it was when she'd gone to sleep and it wasn't nice at all.

"Melody." A voice came from somewhere in the darkness but she couldn't see who it belonged to. It belonged to a grown-up though, she could tell that much because of how deep it was.

"Melody? Are you frightened?"

She nodded. "A little bit, yes. Are you a nasty man?"

There was some laughing then but it echoed a bit and made her feel even more afraid.

"You don't need to be frightened of me. I'm here to

help you."

"Help me go home? I'd like to go home, my mummy and daddy will be worried."

"Oh they are worried, Melody. That's why they sent me to try and help you."

"They know I'm here? I want to go home now, I'm cold." She still couldn't see the owner of the voice and she didn't quite know if he gave her a bad feeling yet or not.

"Not yet, we need to have a chat for a while."

The man said something and came toward her a little. She didn't recognise his voice and she didn't understand what he was saying, it was just too fast.

Her tummy rumbled. "I'm hungry, can I go home?"

Somewhere above was the sound of crying. "Mummy?"

"Shh, Melody. It's important you listen to me without interrupting." The man stepped forward and for the first time she saw just a little bit of his face. It wasn't enough to see him properly but he looked like a kind man. "I'm here to help you, all of you."

He put his hand on her shoulder and this time she got a bad feeling… a really bad feeling.

"Can you hear the scratching?" she said to him. "They don't like me being in here with them. I think this is their home. They don't like it one bit."

He removed his hand before she could see anything other than a rat in the pictures from his mind. The picture shivered and then was gone.

"Have you seen them?" She could hear the same thing in his voice that she had heard in Daddy's voice after she'd done the bad thing.

"I haven't seen any yet but they're in here and they're cross."

"Why do you think they're cross with you, Melody?"

"They're not cross with me. They're cross with you."

The man laughed again and shrank away from her. His laugh wasn't friendly though, it was nervous.

"Can I come out now?" she asked.

The man had gone completely again. "Not yet."

Then a ray of light shone down from above him and he disappeared upward. Had he gone to heaven? Or was she in the other place and he had just come for a visit? The scratching started up again.

"Here, ratty," she called out. If the rats were upset with the man who had given her a bad feeling then they were probably okay to be friends with.

"Ratty?" she called again and held out her hand.

"There's a good boy." She felt the rat's whiskers tickle her fingers. It scurried off again.

Why had they sent her to the dark? The man had said that Mummy and Daddy knew she was here and that they were worried about her. They ought to come and fetch her if they were that worried.

The crying was fainter now but it had definitely sounded like Mummy. Mummy had cried a lot after she'd said and done the bad things. Daddy hadn't cried but his voice trembled a bit when he spoke. He must have been tired; they both must have been after all the talking they did late at night when they thought she was asleep.

But she was awake and she'd heard every single word.

"Here, ratty."

If the rats were cross about it, then she should be too. Very cross.

*

That man had been back lots of times now and each time the bad feeling was worse. He always stayed in the darkness so she couldn't see his face properly and she could tell he was trying really hard to be friendly. It was just that he didn't actually sound very friendly anymore. Most of the time he sounded scared. He always wanted to talk about the bad things she'd said, too. And when she told him she couldn't remember, he got impatient with her. Once he'd told her she could go and see Mummy and Daddy if she told him why she'd said those things.

She wanted to make something up then but making things up was a lie and telling lies was a bad thing to do. The truth was, she couldn't remember saying anything bad. Not once. She could only remember afterwards when Mummy or Daddy were crying or really mad with her.

The time she bumped into those boys and saw what one of them was thinking was bad but that was when she was really little. Was she just two? She might have been and she didn't understand what she'd seen but she knew it was bad. It was evil.

There were others. Boys, girls and grown-ups too. They all had pictures floating about in their brains but only some of them knew they were there and they were the ones who made her feel sick. The worst one was the doctor, though. She'd seen him lots of times and his head was full of the sort of things she imagined nasty men did.

"I need to speak with your daughter alone. Can you wait outside for a moment, I shan't be long."

Mummy and Daddy had asked if it was necessary but the doctor said it was.

"Now, Melody, I want you to tell me why you keep shouting out terrible words. Where have you heard them? Is it from television or perhaps you've heard Mummy or Daddy saying them?"

"I don't know any bad words, only 'bugger' and that's not too bad. Daddy said it when he dropped his cup of tea."

"Any others?"

She'd sat quietly and searched inside her brain for something to say. "I know the word 'fuck' but I don't know what it means." She looked at the doctor for reassurance. He nodded his head.

"That's a very bad word." He leaned a little closer and she could smell minty sweets on his breath.

She felt the beginning of the bad feeling coming along. It was like a train coming down a dark tunnel, like the London Underground.

The doctor with his niece on his lap. She looks just like me but with brown hair. His hand on her knee and a funny feeling in his tummy. Like an excited feeling only slightly different. Like worse and dirty.

"And I know the word 'paedophile'." Then the train

carrying the word arrived at the platform and everything went dark.

Had that been a bad word?

The doctor told Mummy and Daddy there wasn't anything else he could do and they would have to go somewhere else to get help. She'd woken up on the floor with Daddy lifting her up. He looked sad and frightened but he hugged her close and took her out to the car while Mummy stayed and talked to the doctor for a while.

"I don't like him," she'd said to Daddy in the car.

"No, neither do I."

Then Mummy had come back and they'd gone to have an ice cream in the park. But none of them spoke at all for a long time.

*

The rats came more often now. They came to smell the bucket she went to the toilet in and they came after the man had brought her something to eat. They moved quickly but she could see them easily because her eyes were used to the darkness.

She cried less too. Not because she missed her parents any the less but because she knew it wouldn't do her any good.

The man came less, though; the man with the kind face and the frightened voice. He came to bring her food and empty the bucket and when he did he talked about God. She remembered people talking about God before and she remembered being in a church.

A church. People screaming and pointing at her. A feeling of cold terror creeping up her legs as her parents wept.

When was that? Was that something to do with the bad things? Was that why she was here?

There was a man at the front of the church dressed all in black except for his white collar. He was talking slowly and people, including both of her parents, were nodding slowly. Mummy had looked down at her and smiled but it wasn't the warm smile she used to have. The train with the words came rumbling down the track and tried to stop at the platform but she pushed it away, she didn't want to see it.

The man seemed to be looking straight at her. He had dark clouds in his mind. He couldn't understand why everyone was listening to him, not when he was an *adulterer*. That didn't sound like a good thing to be.

And then lots and lots of pictures and words started hurtling toward her from everywhere. There were so many different types of trains and too many tracks and there was no way she could stop them all.

"Mummy? Can we go?" she'd whispered. "I feel sick."

She'd looked down at her again and this time the smile vanished in an instant. She slid away from her, skidding across the wooden pew.

"What's wrong Daddy? Have I said something bad?"

Someone, it might have been Mummy, stifled a scream.

Images of people fucking. Men fucking women, men

fucking men, women fucking women. Pictures of people hitting each other with hammers until their faces were nothing but bloody pulps. Tongues being pulled from mouths with teeth. Knives being pulled across throats. The bad stuff, the really, really bad stuff.

"Mummy, I feel sick." Then she had been sick and as she looked at her cereals for the second time that day, they became something else. The cornflakes became the faces of the people in the church. Each and every one of them snarling and biting at her skin. Each and every one of them was trying to devour her with their tiny snappy teeth.

She'd screamed as loudly as she could and closed her eyes but the trains had arrived and the words were tumbling out onto the platforms. They just kept coming. Brighter, more colourful and vivid and now she could hear other people screaming.

Why were they screaming?

And then she'd opened her eyes and looked for Mummy, she wanted to go home right now but everyone had turned around and they were looking at her. The words came then, words she didn't understand but she had to say them, she had to, or they would burn her guts until they spilled onto the floor like a thousand crawling insects.

She raised her hand and pointed to the man in front. "Wife beater!"

The woman beside him reddened and touched her cheek.

"Sodomite!" She pointed to a man two rows in front.

She marched out of her pew and walked toward the altar. At each row she stopped and looked at the open-mouthed faces staring back at her. Images and words flashed through her brain, forcing themselves out through her mouth. She pulled at her hair, they were bad words, words which she shouldn't know. Words she didn't understand and had never heard before.

"Kiddy-fiddler!" She spat the words at a pale-looking man who tried not to catch her eye.

She gasped as a picture came before her. It was of a woman hacking at a man's neck with a small silver knife. On and on she hacked until his head hung limply from the side. The man was her husband but it was not the man whose hand she held now, in this church.

"Murderer," she said calmly and walked on.

Another woman, a sad woman, plunged a knife into another man's chest while someone laughed in the background. It was too faint to see properly, not like the others.

"Fuck, fuck, fuck," she chanted as her purple glittery shoes tip-tapped across the flagstones, past the font and to the foot of the pulpit stairs. And down he came until he stood before her, the man whose letters spelled A-D-U-L-T-E-R-E-R in bright red across his face.

"Faithless!" she screamed as loudly as she could and the words burned on the way out of her mouth.

The vicar looked away. He couldn't stand to look at her, he couldn't bear to see what was in her eyes.

"Adulterer," she whispered.

He looked directly at her and then away again. He looked directly at her Mummy.

She followed his stare and looked at her Mummy too. The same words were written across her head, and in red felt-tip pen. "Adulterer?"

Then a burning sensation had crept up the back of her neck and plucked at the skin behind her ear. Her skin started to pull tighter and tighter across her face until she thought it might actually rip away from her skull.

"Daddy?" She was aware of falling and of screaming. There was screaming everywhere and the loudest voice was her own. It came from somewhere deep inside the dark and terrifying cave her mind had become.

9

Children. Stokes had always wanted children. So why hadn't he had any? Twice Jo had conceived and twice things had gone bad, really bad.

The first time, he'd lifted her sobbing from the bed and put her in a warm bath. He'd washed her hair and wiped the blood from her thighs. He'd stripped the sheets and turned the mattress but neither of them had slept a wink. How could they? How was anyone supposed to sleep after that? How was anyone supposed to sleep when they were sharing a bed with their dead child? Even if it was only a collection of cells.

The next day he'd taken the mattress, the sheets and the duvet outside and burned them. He'd stared into the flames and watched silently as they stripped any signs of the baby's existence from the world.

Jo had wept for days; of course she had. But he hadn't, he'd just held onto her. Then eventually the crying stopped and he'd wanted to try again, they both had. And that was a mistake, especially so soon afterwards.

At first he thought he'd pissed the bed. A lovely warm feeling had spread up his legs and along his thighs until his half-sleep delirium came crashing to earth with a terrible and decisive thud.

"Jo?" he'd whispered. Half of her face had been illuminated by the street light coming in through a crack in the curtains.

"Jo?" He'd gently shaken her cold and naked shoulder. "Jo, I think something bad has happened."

She'd stirred and rolled over to face him. "What is it, Jim? Why are you waking me up?" Her eyes had been closed but he couldn't say a word more. Words didn't seem to be adequate. Then her sleep-stunned body had woken up as the warmth spread along her thighs too.

"Jim?" Her voice had pleaded with him. "Jim?"

All he could do was shake his head and throw back the covers. The police officer had a job to do. He needed to sort the situation. He needed to switch on and be the man he was at work. Jo had reached for the lamp but he stopped her.

"No," he'd said simply. He slipped his arms under her and lifted her out of the bed. She let out a little whimper that nearly broke his heart there and then.

"I'll run a nice hot bath." He carried her to the bathroom. "Just keep your eyes on me, sweetheart. Don't look down." In truth he needed to keep his eyes on her too. He didn't want to look at the dark shadow that covered the lower half of her body. And they sat there on the edge of the bath just staring at each other while the steam rose around them. They sat in silence. And then he'd lifted her in and washed her again. The water had turned darker and darker until it was as black as tar.

There had been so much blood, so much, and it just wouldn't stop coming.

"Don't leave me, Jim. I'm frightened."

"I'm going to fetch your robe and then we'll go to the hospital." The policeman needed to get the casualty to the hospital.

Jo had kept her eyes on him all the way to the hospital and hadn't looked down, not once. But he'd been driving and then he'd been speaking to the nurse and then to the doctor. Not once had he looked at her, not once had he taken her hand and said, *"It'll be all right, Jo. Everything will be all right."*

Why?

Because he was a shit?

No, not because he was a shit but because the tiny fissures which were now great crevasses had already started opening up inside his mind. If he'd looked at her, if he'd looked deep into Jo's eyes, he would've seen them reflected back at him and he didn't care to see them.

He'd burned the mattress again. He would've burned the whole damned house down if he could find enough petrol to do the job. He would've taken a knife to Jesus Christ and sliced him up good and fine if he could've found him. Instead he stood in silence and watched as the flames licked at the blood-soaked mattress and devoured his unborn child for the second time.

When at last the flames died down leaving only a collection of warped springs, he turned his head to the early morning sky.

"Fuck you." His voice was barely audible. It was less than a whisper, almost a breath and the only ones who heard it were the angels and God himself and they chose not to reply.

How would it have been if things had been different? If Jo had managed to hold onto the babies, would they still be together? There was no way of answering that. But he'd pondered it nevertheless. And what would their children be like? He'd imagined a boy and a girl with about a year between them. They never got as far as talking about names but secretly he'd always loved the name Daisy. Daisy Stokes had a nice ring to it. She'd be pretty too, just like her mum and full of beans. And the boy? What would he be called? Perhaps he'd just have a good look at him when he was born to decide that. He'd be cheeky though, not in a rude or spoilt way, just charming and disarming. He'd met enough characters like that in his lifetime to know they were the ones who got away with anything and everything and yet you couldn't help loving them for it. One day all four of them would take a tent down to Cornwall and catch crabs in the rock-pools. One day…

"Fuck you." Stokes looked out over the lake and watched the lights on the far side of the lake twinkle in the dusk. How long had he been there, caught up in some sick daydream? His head was pounding. He hadn't drunk or eaten anything all day and his head was complaining about it.

He levered himself out of the recliner and shuffled into the kitchen. A box of paracetamol lay open on the worktop. He switched the light on in the extractor hood and pushed four out of the blister pack. Even getting a glass out of the cupboard felt like too much effort so he stretched his head under the tap. He swallowed the tablets and allowed the water to wash over his face. It wasn't safe to move until the need to vomit had passed but the water felt good on his skin, and if it wasn't for the cramp building in his neck he might have stayed longer.

He opened the cupboard and took a packet of noodles out.

"Thai Chicken," he muttered and dropped them on the floor.

Water was one thing but food was another entirely. He turned and looked at the stairs and then back at the recliner. Spending another night in the chair couldn't possibly make him feel any worse. He walked slowly back and pulled the duvet around his naked body. No, he was pretty sure he couldn't feel any worse even if he was buried alive.

Was this punishment for something? Was this last year the wrath of God? It hardly seemed fair if it was. He'd told God to fuck off twice and the last time was a minute ago, in any case both times were entirely justified. It certainly didn't merit this sort of treatment anyway. Or was that the problem? Was it the lack of communication that had brought this on? Wind rattled the patio doors making him jump.

"I'm sorry."

He waited for a moment and laughed. "I was hoping for a reprieve if I apologised." He laughed again and even to his own ears it sounded wrong.

"Like a lunatic," he whispered and was instantly gripped by a terrible spasm of pain in his abdomen. It twisted him in the chair and made the pain in his head intensify by a factor of one thousand.

"I said I'm sorry!" he gasped.

A few moments later it subsided and allowed him to flop back again. He took several deep breaths and closed his eyes. He didn't fancy too many more of those episodes this side of death.

"I'll just sit here and keep quiet."

Scretch, scretch, scretch.

"I can hear you behind me and when I get back to fighting fitness, we'll have round two, my dear rodent housemates."

A light and warm breeze tickled the back of his neck pleasantly. He was sure none of the windows were open, at least he didn't think he'd opened any in the last few days. Wherever it was coming from, it was okay by him because it was comforting somehow.

He stretched his neck and rotated it until he heard a loud crack. It sent a tiny shock down his spine and forced his eyes open.

It was pitch black outside now and the little light from

the kitchen bounced his own image back like a mirror. The doors moved a little in the wind and distorted his face, twisting it into the visage of an old man. He stared at it intently for a while until he no longer recognised it as his own.

The breeze tickled his neck again and this time it sent a shiver down his spine. Where was it coming fr…

He moved forward in his chair a little. He was imagining it, he had to be. A little girl was standing outside the doors looking in at him. Her shoulder-length hair was the colour of honey and her smile was as beautiful as any he'd seen. Her smart little purple dress didn't move an inch in the wind. She looked like she was going to a party. She must belong to one of the villagers who he'd never met. None of them were young enough to have a daughter of this age. Perhaps a grandchild then? But why was she outside on a night like this? She couldn't be much more than seven or eight at the most. No-one should be walking by the lake on a night like this, especially not a little girl.

The hair on the back of his neck stood up. How could he see her so clearly when it was pitch black outside? He felt the breeze on his neck again, warm and comforting, like… like what? Not like a breeze at all but like the gentle heat of another person's breath on his skin… of someone standing behind him. And why was she looking down at him, from over his shoulder, and not at him through the window?

He flicked his head around, almost giving himself

whiplash, but the room was empty, completely empty. He turned almost as quickly back to the doors but all that remained was his own decrepit and contorted face.

He shrugged and edged back into his chair. It wasn't the first time he'd seen things, in fact it seemed that all he had been doing for the last year was seeing things. Besides, after spending the last year with the psycho-bitch-from-hell snapping at him, the little girl was a welcome new face.

There had been no threat from her, no gnashing of teeth or cursing. She'd just stood there looking down at him. He touched the shoulder over which she'd been standing. Was it just part of the fever or was it his damaged brain conjuring up yet more nastiness?

He lifted his hand from his shoulder. No, this felt different somehow. The breath on his neck had been warm and tender, not savage and intense.

"Hello?" He cocked his ear and listened. Wind rattled at the door but there was nothing else, not even the rats answered.

"Little girl, are you there?" He waited again and then laughed. "Don't be so ridiculous, Stokes."

He couldn't wait to get rid of Natalie and yet here he was courting another mirage. His brain was addled but not so badly as to invite another third party to play fiddlesticks with his mind. No, this was nothing more than a well-timed counter-balance to make up for Natalie finally being put to bed.

He didn't know why he was so sure that she'd gone for good but he was. Perhaps it was the writing on the floor that he'd also imagined? Yes, that was it. At last he'd turned that corner he always promised himself was just over the next hill. So what if he saw a girl on his shoulder from time to time? Eventually she'd go too and he'd be back to his old self again. Maybe he'd meet someone he could have children with? Now there was something to aim for.

"New start, Stokesy. New start."

His body was wracked by another spasm of pain. It burst from the wound in his torso and infected his entire body like a thousand angry hornet stings.

He dug his nails into the leather arms of the recliner and waited for it to pass. It was a long time coming but when it did he let out a grunt. He loosened the towel but stopped short of disturbing it too much. He couldn't see much but judging from the towel it had been bleeding again. He pushed the dirty towel back over it, sending a slightly sweet smell wafting up to him. He really ought to get over to the hospital in the next couple of days. He pulled the duvet around his body again and reclined the chair to the horizontal. There was no point in rushing things, he needed to be fit again before he attempted the journey.

"New start, Stokesy. New start."

He closed his eyes and fell asleep instantly.

*

Were his eyes open or was it just another bad dream? Maybe he'd gone blind, now wouldn't that just ice the cake. He rubbed his face to make sure his eyes weren't still shut. What new trick was this? He blinked rapidly and caught the odd sliver of light flashing across his vision. Shards of faint sunlight pierced the darkness and struck the earth like daggers. He looked up at the floorboards above his head. He knew where he was, and it wasn't just the smell of ammonia that told him that. He was in the pit again, but how on earth had he got there?

Christ, he felt bad. A fire had been burning steadily in his belly but now it felt like a raging furnace had been lit. He groaned and sat up. He remembered lying down on the recliner and that beautiful brief moment before sleep finally took him, but that was all. Certainly not slipping into the pit for a nap anyway.

His mouth was parched and it tasted bad. No, not just bad but sour and dusty. He wiped his mouth with the back of his hand and looked at it. A dark smear covered the skin but he didn't need to see it to know there was dirt in his mouth. He gathered as much saliva as he could manage and spat between his legs. The soil was laced with rat piss and crap and God alone knew what else. Was it Weil's disease that was carried on rat's urine? It was a small consolation that it was difficult to imagine feeling any worse than he did right now. All he needed at that very minute was Natalie to come storming into the pit.

But she was gone, right? He came to that conclusion last night, right about the same time he saw the little girl outside... right about the same time he realised she was actually standing behind him, breathing gently on the back of his neck. He laughed to himself. If anyone could hear his thoughts, if anyone could see the state of him right now, they would have him committed. No questions asked.

"As comfortable as you've made me feel, I really must be going." He dragged himself into a crouch and shuffled toward where he thought the hatch must be. It was difficult to get his bearings in the semi-darkness though. The shafts of light were sporadic where the floorboards had shrunk and warped over time and what little light came through was lessened by the time of year.

He reached up and pushed against the boards as he moved, trying to locate the loose square where the hatch had been cut. Every so often he thought he'd found it and pushed against the wood harder. The effort sent a crushing spasm of agony through his body, causing him to call out. His heart raced and a growing sense of panic started to wriggle about in his toes. He knew it wouldn't be long before it started slithering up his legs past his crotch and into his guts. How the hell had he got down there?

It felt as if he were wandering deeper and deeper into a thick forest. The kind of place which only existed in fairy tales and nightmares. Exactly the kind of place which he seemed to be inhabiting nearly all the time now.

He was totally disoriented and he stopped. Somewhere he could hear the faint quacks of the ducks on Lake Stormark but the sound reverberated around the space until its source was lost completely. He gritted his teeth and banged on the floorboards in anger. He was naked and trapped in a hell-hole beneath his own home. He kicked at the dirt beneath his toes.

"Shit!" He hopped backward away from whatever he'd just kicked.

His eyes had adjusted to the darkness but still they weren't quite good enough to see distinct shapes, particularly in this darker area where there were no light shafts to help. His foot had connected with something wet, something which had yielded to his kick and squelched beneath his toes. His first thought was that he'd just toe-punted a rat across the floor but that wasn't right. Even if it were dead, it wasn't right.

He stepped forward and dropped to his knees. He couldn't see anything obvious but what exactly was he looking for? He reached forward and moved his arms in arcs in front of his body, scraping the top layer of soil away. It was much wetter here than elsewhere in the space.

There it was again. The tips of his fingers brushed against something unpleasant but it wasn't a rat, not unless it was hairless and made out of soggy cardboard. He scrambled toward it and tried to lift it but its integrity was shot to pieces and it almost fell between his fingers.

He crouched over it and stared for a moment. It was a shoebox, as simple and unassuming as that, yet it was strangely out of place. There was nothing else down here at all, nothing except the rats and they didn't need footwear.

He should open it and look inside, he knew he should, but somehow it didn't feel right. The cottage was his but this wasn't. This belonged to someone else.

He gently pushed it to one side and looked about. If the ground was wetter over here then he had to be closer to the lake, which meant the hatch had to be over on the other side somewhere. A surge of relief swept over him and for a moment he thought he might cry. Tears pooled in the corners of his eyes but he wiped them away with a grubby fist before they could fall.

"Daddy, are you there, Daddy?"

Stokes spun around. It sounded like someone had whispered behind him.

"Daddy, can I come out now?"

There it was again but this time it came from the other side of the cellar.

"Daddy, I'm frightened, please take me home."

He turned again and this time looked straight at the box. He needed to get out of there and he needed to take the box with him. He didn't know why exactly but he was sure of it, the feeling was as sure as anything he'd ever felt in his life.

He scooped the box up as gently as he could and gathered it to his chest. He could feel the cold damp of the soaked cardboard crawling across the skin. If he walked in a straight line, sooner or later he'd walk head-first into the stone foundation of his house. He retched and allowed the bile to fall in yo-yo string from his mouth. It clung to his lower lip for a second and fell onto his toes. He couldn't wipe it away, if he took a hand away from the box he might drop it and that was a bad idea. He shuffled his toes into the dirt and rubbed it away.

"Best foot forward."

*

He pushed the box up first and clambered back into the cottage. It wasn't a bright day by any means but he was forced to squint as his eyes readjusted to the light. He doubted whether it had ever been a decent day but now as he looked out of the rain-splashed doors, it was drawing to a close. He shivered as a chill ran through his body. His body clock was all over the place and as for his internal thermostat, well that was just about on its last legs.

There was only one place he wanted to be right now – in bed. He scooped up the box and pulled it to his chest. It had faded green writing on one side – 'Clarks'. At one time or another, every kid in his school had owned a pair of Clarks shoes. It was probably the same in every school across the country. He plodded up the stairs, his filthy feet living prints as he went. Yep, he was going to put the box right next to him in bed and when he'd taken a nap he was going to have a look inside.

*

Scretch, scretch, screttttccchhh.

The rats were in bed with him now, scuttling about and chewing the bed, the sheets and for all he knew, his toes too. The last thought pulled him out of the nap instantly.

"Get off me!" he shouted and sat bolt upright. There

were no rats nibbling at his toes but the bed was covered in mud and rat shit and probably all sorts of other unsavoury substances. What had he been dreaming of this time? He hadn't been asleep long, not properly anyway but there had been a dream in there somewhere, he just couldn't quite tease it out.

The makeshift bandage on his torso was almost black and the tape holding it in place was curling up at the edges. He pulled it off slowly and winced at the odour coming from the wound. It was getting worse, there might be some poisoning starting. The narrow strip of clean skin where the towel had stopped the dirt penetrating looked odd to him, like it shouldn't be there. It should look the same as the rest of his body. Maybe not.

He pushed the skin on either side of the wound forcing thick green pus upward and out onto his thigh. He looked at it for a moment then scooped it up on the tip of his finger. Was this what was inside of him now? Was this all that was left? He sniffed it then wiped it on the sheet beside him.

The shoe box. That was right, he'd bought the shoe box up from the pit.

Scretch, scretch, scretch.

Had the rats got in there somehow? He tapped on the lid gently. It had started to dry out but it would never hold a pair of shoes again.

Scretch, scretch, scretch. The noise grew louder.

He tapped on the lid again. "Come out, come out, wherever you are." He flicked it off with his forefinger and edged away from it. No rats came filing out.

Scretch, scretch, scretch. It was almost too loud now and it was starting to give him another headache.

He pushed the side of the box with his finger but it was wet and his finger went straight through. There had to be a rat in there, there just had to be, and it had to be chewing on a brick judging by the noise it was making. Stokes grabbed the box and shook it. That signalled the end of its integrity and it collapsed completely. He could feel his irritation starting to bubble over into a steady rage.

Scretch, scretch, scretch. The sound was deafening now. He couldn't take anymore, he raised his hands above his head and smashed them into what was left of the box. The sound stopped immediately.

Was that crying somewhere? He stopped and listened. No, it must have been a bird on the lake.

He pushed the lid to one side and stared utterly perplexed at what was now lying on his bed.

"Hair."

He reached out and took it in his hands. It was honey-coloured, just like… just like the girl who'd been watching him from outside, or was it inside? It didn't matter, it was the same colour. He held it to his nose and inhaled. It smelled of how he imagined the clouds would smell, just like a little girl's hair should smell. It was unfortunate that the rats had got into the box and crapped in there. The shrivelled black dots were literally everywhere.

He reached down and took another clump in his hand. What was this? Little gems, pure little ivory gems, had been secreted amongst the golden strands. It was as beautiful as any jewellery imaginable. Stokes teased one out. The ivory wasn't quite as pure as he'd first thought, in fact one end was covered in a dark stain and the other end was ground down in a jagged mess. It was sharp enough to draw blood.

One by one he pulled them out of the hair until he had a full set of twenty teeth gathered around him on the bed. They were beautiful, absolutely exquisite, and he was held in a thrall by each and every one of them. Even the ones which had been ground down into savage little spikes.

Scretch, scretch, scretch.

Were they talking to him?

10

The bad words had seemed to come tumbling from her mouth and run across the floor. The words looked like the nest of woodlice she'd disturbed in the garden last summer. They were ugly and they made her feel sick.

After the church it was as if nobody she knew could bear to look at her anymore, at least not in the daylight. Once or twice she'd seen words written across Mummy's face but they were black and even more scary than the red letters. They looked like they might crawl off Mummy's face and eat someone's eyes out. Mummy must have seen the look on her face when she saw the letters too, because she started to turn her head away whenever she spoke to her now.

Both of them still came in to kiss her night-night though, even if it was when they thought she was fast asleep. Daddy spoke to her then too. His face was always so close to hers that she could smell his breath; it smelled hot and spicy.

"I love you, Melody." He always started that way, in a soft whisper which made her want to giggle. Then he'd start telling her about what he'd done that day and how much he missed seeing her smile. But that wasn't true because she was always smiling, it was just that they didn't look at her to see it anymore. Then he would kiss her on the forehead and his whiskers would tickle her skin, not too much but just enough to make her remember how things were before the bad words kept pushing their way out. The worst bit was when she could hear his voice change slightly and a teardrop would land on her cheek. She wanted to wipe it away but if she did then he'd know she wasn't asleep and things would go back to how they were during the daytime. Mostly she just wanted to throw her arms around him and let him pick her up and hold her against him. He never did that, not now. Neither of them did.

She'd had a comfortable bed then.

She wasn't afraid of the rats or of the darkness now. She couldn't remember when that had changed but she was glad it had. She chased them sometimes. It was like a game, like the games of chase she used to play at school with the other children. They weren't like the children though, the rats couldn't shout and laugh and they didn't have any letters written across their heads, ever. The rats seemed to enjoy it anyway and they weren't afraid of her either.

Sometimes they would sit in her lap and bring her bits of their food. It wasn't nice though, they liked to eat rotten things that smelled bad. They liked bones too. They chewed them with their sharp little teeth, passing them from side to side with their cold little fingers.

She liked to do impressions of them and chomp her teeth together while they stared at her. Her mouth ached a lot and some of her teeth felt a bit soft when she ground them together. She couldn't stop it though because the rats liked it and they were her friends.

Scretch, scretch, scretch. That was the sound it made and more of her friends came to see her when she made her teeth make the sound. She was like the Pied Piper of Hamelin, only she wasn't taking them away but bringing them closer.

That man still came every day too. How long had she been down here? She should start counting each day when he came, that way she would know. He still gave her a bad feeling but she couldn't see any words on his face, and that was okay because she was sure that was what had sent her down here in the first place. His voice was familiar though, she was sure she'd heard it before.

"Melody, do you know what a paedophile is?"

"No I don't but it isn't a good thing to be."

"And why do you say that?" His voice irritated her. He was trying to sound like a teacher but he wasn't one. She could tell.

"Because when I saw it on the doctor's face, the letters were crawling about like they were spiders. I don't like spiders so the rats eat them all."

The man had looked around, she saw his head move

quickly from side to side. This made her smile.

"And that's it? That's all?"

"Yep, that's it."

"And these words, you actually saw them? They weren't words you've heard on television or at school?"

"Of course I saw them. He's a paedophile, isn't he?"

"No, Melody, he isn't. He was trying to help you."

"Well he soon will be." She laughed but was it funny? She didn't really know.

"What? What do you mean by that?"

"Well, he might not be now but he will be soon. The words said so. Just like you, you'll be an adulterer soon, just like Mummy."

"How… What on earth are you saying, Melody? I don't understand you." She could hear a tremble in his voice and it made her feel good.

She shrugged. "The words don't lie, Mr Vicar. They don't ever lie." She knew who he was now, his voice had given it away.

"Melody, you're not making any sense."

"I am. The words are always true. Sometimes there's pictures too but only if they've already done what the words say. I don't understand them most of the time but sometimes they make me feel bad."

"Bad? In what way?"

"You make me feel bad." She peered into the darkness to try and see him but it was too dark. "People who make me feel bad are nearly always thinking about doing something nasty. I can't see any words then."

"Me? Why? I'm not doing anything except talking to you, Melody. I'm not thinking about doing anything bad."

She ignored his question, she didn't know how to answer him. "What's a faithless person?"

He was quiet for a long time. "It's someone who doesn't believe in anything."

"Like God?"

"Yes, like God."

"Are you faithless, Vicar?"

She heard him shift his position in the dirt. He was feeling uncomfortable talking about it and that was good.

"No, Melody. I'm a vicar and it's important that I have faith. What about you? What do you think about God?"

She ignored him again. "I think that's the bad thing you've been thinking about."

He laughed but it wasn't a funny laugh, it was a nervous laugh. "You're not very well, Melody. You know that, don't you?"

"Being faithless would be a very bad thing, especially for you. I think it might hurt quite a lot."

"Be quiet!" his voice boomed. "When I look at you, do you know what I see? Do you know what words I see painted across your head?"

She didn't answer. He was giving her a really bad feeling now, like he wanted to do something really bad, probably worse than being faithless.

"Well do you?" he shouted again.

"You can't see anything," she whispered.

"I see the words, sick, ill, mean, spiteful and alone!"

They were both quiet for a while. The Vicar was so quiet that she started to think he'd gone away again. But then she heard a sniff. "I'm sorry, Melody. I shouldn't have said those things. I don't see anything other than a little girl, a frightened little girl."

"I'm not frightened. Not anymore."

"You frighten other people though, you know that too, don't you?"

"I don't care about them, I only care about Mummy and Daddy. Do I frighten them?" She knew the answer to that but she wanted someone else to say it to her.

"Sometimes, yes you do."

She didn't want to think about that. If she thought about Mummy and Daddy then she would cry.

"Is that why I'm here? Is it because everyone's afraid of me?"

The Vicar didn't answer.

"Will I see Mummy and Daddy again?"

He didn't answer and started sliding away from her. She knew the answer to that question too.

"Why do I only see bad words?"

"I don't know, Melody." His voice was faint but she could tell he was crying.

Why did she only see bad words? Why couldn't she see the nice things that were written across people's faces? Surely not everyone had nasty things inside them. Perhaps the bad things were stronger than the good things and the good words couldn't get out.

She pulled her legs up to her chest and pulled at her hair. Mummy used to brush her hair all the time and she always said how beautiful it was. She pulled a clump out and twisted it along her finger. She really ought to have somewhere to put it all, somewhere like a keepsake box. Yes, that would be perfect.

Why did she only see the bad words?

She knew the words written across her own face were worse than the ones the Vicar had said. He was just making that lot up because there was only one word written across her face and it was in bright red. It said DEAD.

*

Everybody dies. That's what the kids in the playground had told her. Everybody dies sometime, nobody lives forever. But she couldn't see it, at least not then. She was just a little girl and if everybody died, like they said, then it wasn't until they were really old; much older than Mummy and Daddy. Perhaps then, people died, if they had to.

She'd asked Daddy about it, before things went bad, and he'd looked up from his paper and smiled at her. "It's just how life works, sweetheart. It happens all the time." He'd seen how worried she looked at his answer so he'd scooped her up and held her to his chest. She'd heard his heart beating, *dum dum, dum dum.*

"Not you though, Daddy. You're never going to die, are you?"

She'd heard him laugh then and it had been a happy sound. It was the sound he used to make.

She squeezed her eyes shut and tried to picture his face. It was hard but gradually his face appeared in the darkness.

"Am I dead, Daddy? Am I actually dead?" she whispered to herself.

But she knew she wasn't, not really. The words on her head said she was but they weren't true. She wasn't dead yet but she might as well have been.

Scretch, scretch, scretch. It felt good to rub her teeth together and even better when one of them dropped into her lap. If she licked the blood off the bottom, it was like a little jewel. If she'd been able to find a piece of string she might have made a necklace like one of Mummy's. She hadn't been able to find any but she had found an old shoe box. Inside it there was treasure, real treasure. She'd put spun gold and milky pearls as big as... well, as little girl's teeth. She needed to keep it all because Mummy would want to see it. Mummy would want to keep it for her own keepsake.

She rubbed her hand over her head. There wasn't much left now, it felt like there were just a few loose strands here and there. Never mind, when she got out, the sunshine would help her grow some more. Did the sunshine help to grow teeth as well?

She hated that man, the Vicar. She thought she might be close to hating Mummy and Daddy too. Why didn't they just come and get her? Why did they let this man keep her here? He was a nasty man which meant they were pretty nasty too.

Some of the rats had given birth to babies. She knew that because they made squeaking noises all the time. Not the loud noises the big ones made but little whimpering cries that were both sweet and annoying at the same time. She knew where they all lived but it was way over in the corner and the smell was bad, so bad that it made her cough and her eyes water.

Those babies had mummies and daddies. She didn't, not anymore.

She listened to the sound of the baby rats and the occasional duck outside.

"Shut up!" She pressed her hands to her ears but she could still hear them.

"Shut up, shut up, shut up!" She scampered across the dirt toward the rats' nest. Why should they have nice mummies and daddies who looked after them? Why should they when she didn't have anyone?

She pushed her hand into the bundle of twigs and grass and grabbed something small and warm between her fingers. It wriggled a bit as she pulled her hand free but it didn't struggle as much as she'd thought it might. The baby rat didn't have any hair at all and it felt a bit funny.

She held it up to her face and looked into its eyes. They were like little black jewels. Not nearly as pretty as her own little pearls but they were nice all the same.

Animals never had any words written across their foreheads but why would they? They didn't know anything, they probably didn't even know what dying was.

She pushed her finger into the rat's eye. It started to struggle and make a really horrible squealing noise but she didn't stop. She wanted the lovely looking gems for her own box, they would look beautiful beside her own collection. Mummy would be so pleased.

*

There were footsteps on the boards directly above her head. She listened carefully to the tip tap sound. It was strange to hear more than one set of steps but there were definitely two people up there. There might even be three. Nobody ever came to visit the Vicar. She doubted whether he had any friends at all but why would someone like that know anyone who loved him? Who would want to come to his house for a cup of tea? No, it was strange all right.

Her heart leapt. Was it Mummy and Daddy come to collect her at last? Perhaps she was better now? Yes that was it, she was all better and they were going to take her back home. As soon as she got in she was going to jump on her bed and bounce up and down with happiness. That was right after she'd wrapped her arms around them both and said sorry for whatever it was she'd said or done.

She scrambled across the floor and grabbed the shoe box. The rat's eyes didn't last long but there were plenty of babies and when one lot were gone another lot came around just like that. She opened the box and looked inside.

"Twenty." She could count all the way to… what was the big number? She couldn't quite remember but twenty was easy and that was how many pearls there were in the box. She closed it quickly in case the spun gold escaped.

"Mummy?" she called gently in case it wasn't Mummy and it was another nasty man.

She waited and listened for the footsteps again.

"Daddy?"

The hatch opened on the far side of the room and allowed a solid beam of light to push through the darkness. This usually signalled that the Vicar was coming down to talk to her. Today she wasn't in her usual place though, she wasn't sitting hunched up on the mattress. Today she was out of view, in the damp and dark recess of the cave she knew better than anyone.

"Melody?" She heard his voice but he was still out of sight. "Melody? Are you there?"

She opened her mouth to speak but didn't make a sound.

"Melody, can you come to the hatch so I can see you."

He came down to see her less and less now. Was he bored with her or just frightened?

"I've got Mummy and Daddy here, would you like to see them?"

She dropped the box and leapt toward the light. At last! She knew they wouldn't forget her.

"Mummy!" she called and stumbled into the spotlight.

A scream nearly made her jump back into the darkness.

"Mummy?" She'd heard Mummy scream before and she recognised her voice.

She tried to look up into the light but it was like

staring straight into the sun. She could see nothing.

"What is it? Can I come out now, I've been good and I'm all better."

There was a loud sob followed by a wail.

"I can't see you. Daddy, are you there too?"

The sound of the hatch falling into place cast her into darkness again. She looked up at the knots of wood on the hatch and pressed her fingers against them. Perhaps the Vicar was playing a trick on her and it wasn't really Mummy and Daddy. Well, if that was how he wanted to play then she might have a trick or two up her own sleeve.

She could hear raised voices in the room upstairs. Why had they screamed when they saw her? She was pretty, at least that's what Daddy always said. Perhaps they had seen a rat? But that was just silly because the rats were fine once you got used to them. She crawled back to the box and opened the lid. The little black gems looked more like specks of dirt now. It was a shame they didn't last very long.

The light had hurt her eyes so much, it felt like they were being burned. Did she really want to go back out there? It was a place where she heard and saw things which weren't nice and those things usually got her into trouble. Down here she couldn't see any words, none at all and that suited her just fine. She didn't frighten anymore, at least nobody except the Vicar and he was just a silly fool. She didn't have to pretend to be asleep so Daddy wouldn't look at her like he didn't understand her anymore. If she had to listen to Mummy crying every day again then she might rip her own ears off. No, down here there was none of that. Down here was safe.

She tucked the box under her armpit and scampered back to the mattress. The Vicar was a silly fool but he was also nasty and mean. Fancy tricking her like that. She'd have a think and see what she could do to him in return. It would be something he didn't like, something he really didn't like.

"One, two, three…" She counted her pearls again.

11

Dead. It was written on the Velux window, in bright red pen.

"Dead." Stokes stared at the word. Spots of rain were falling onto the window but the letters weren't smudging. It was written on the inside.

"Dead," he repeated it. Slowly the letters ran down the window in spidery lines until there was nothing left there at all.

He wasn't dead, he knew that. The nauseating pain in his side was evidence of his existence. Unless he was dead and this was hell?

He picked the tape off his torso and pulled the towel aside completely. He was greeted by a putrid stench which caused him to retch. If at all possible, the smell was worse than the pain. It needed some air, that was all. An hour or two without the stinking towel would sort it out.

He swung his feet off the bed. What time was it? He wrapped his fingers around his wrist. He was sure he'd had a watch yesterday, or was it the day before? It didn't really matter what time it was anyway, he didn't have anywhere to go, not unless he wanted to.

Fresh air, that was what he needed. Fresh air and a walk down to the lake. He stood up and felt the bedroom do a three-sixty around him before it stopped. He should eat something before he attempted to go for a stroll.

He slipped on his jeans, ignoring the filth he was covered in. No-one would see him, nobody else would be out on a day like this.

Scretch, scretch, scretch.

He turned around and looked at the teeth and hair on the bed. The hair was still as beautiful as ever. Golden honey seemed to run through it in a sumptuous and oozing river. He'd kept it on the pillow beside him as he'd fallen asleep. He remembered staring at it, utterly transfixed, as his eyes finally closed.

He looked down at his hand and opened his clenched fist. Five tiny teeth, jagged and worn, had left indentations all over his palm. He tightened his fist around them again and felt the bite of one of the jagged edges dig into his skin before he dropped them into his jeans pocket.

Rain hammered on the roof window, it was coming down so hard and fast that it was almost keeping pace with the thumping of his heart. Yes, this was a good day for a walk down to the water. It was the sort of day that washed your troubles away.

He grabbed the handrail and made his way slowly down the stairs. He felt weak but all things considered, not too bad. Wasn't there a half-eaten steak in the house somewhere? He needed protein to make himself stronger and he remembered eating only a small part of a steak he'd cooked yesterday, or was it the day before? It was recently anyway, the days seemed to be merging into one at the moment. He reached into the bag under the sink and pulled out the meat. He sniffed it and stuffed it into his mouth. If he could keep it down then it would do him the world of good.

He turned and stopped; the meat hung from his mouth like a giant deformed tongue.

"Hello?" he whispered.

The little girl stood on top of the hatch. She said nothing but stared back at him.

Stokes allowed the steak to fall from his mouth and land on his feet. He dug into his pocket and brought out the teeth.

"You can have them if you want. They're very pretty, just like you." He offered them to her.

He thought he saw a flicker of a smile on her rose-bud lips and then she was gone.

"Am I dead?" he shouted, and then added in a whisper, "Are you?"

He shrugged and grabbed the steak from the top of his foot where it had landed. "Does it matter?"

*

He stood on the foreshore and looked down at his bare feet. A shoal of dying fish convulsed in the sand and flapped their tails at his skin as they took their last desperate breaths. Weak grey light reflected off their scales and briefly gave them their lives back before the sun disappeared behind the clouds. He flicked one back into the water with his toes.

The rain pounded on his skin in a wonderful, rhythmic percussion. It washed over the wound and crept inside the gaping flesh where it cooled the burning tissue. He stretched his arms out to either side and closed his eyes. There was nothing except for the exquisite sound of the rain. It smashed into the lake and thrashed into the earth with a brutal intention that signalled the wishes of mother nature. This was all hers and she would do with it as she wished. She could do with him whatever she wanted too.

He roared with all his might. It was a low sound, almost a growl, it shocked him and at the same time excited him. He could stay like this forever, just him and the earth in perfect savage harmony.

"Jim?"

He turned slowly to the side and opened his eyes.

"Jim, are you okay?"

He stared silently at the man facing him and although he knew it was someone he should know, he didn't recognise him. No, that wasn't quite right. He couldn't recognise him. Red paint covered his face and dripped off the point of his chin in a steady and unrelenting stream.

"Jim? What's wrong?"

Stokes took a step away. Was it paint or blood? "I'm sorry," he muttered and wiped his eyes. Some of the mud that caked his face and hair was running into his eyes.

"It's me."

Slowly the paint succumbed to the rain and ran from his face in thick crimson rivulets. It was Peter.

"Jesus." He pointed at Stokes's stomach. "What've you done?"

Stokes looked down at the wound and ran his finger around the lesion. Blood gathered briefly on his finger before the rain washed it away. "Nothing." The wound itself didn't hurt much anymore but his thighs, groin and ribs were howling like mad. He was angry, not because Peter had disturbed the moment but because he'd reminded him of the pain.

"It doesn't look like nothing. Have you been rolling around in the mud? You're absolutely plastered in it."

"It's nothing," Stokes repeated. "What do you want?"

His tone had clearly shocked Peter who said nothing for a moment. "I was just passing and I thought I'd come and see you. It's a good job by the look of you."

A word, daubed in bright red flashed across Peter's face. It said 'Liar'.

Stokes shook his head and the word was gone. "I'm fine. I fell that's all."

"Are you sure? You look like shit, pardon the language."

"I'm fucking fine, if you'll pardon mine." He watched the other man's face for a reaction but there was none.

"Okay, I get the message." He walked past Stokes, along the edge of the lake, back toward the village.

Stokes felt bad. The cool rain had given him a lucidity he hadn't felt for a while. This wasn't him, any more than it had been him at the DIY store in town. "Sorry!" he called after Peter. The other man didn't turn but raised his hand in acknowledgement.

Stokes ran after him. His legs complained bitterly but they responded. He caught up with Peter and put his hand on his shoulder. Peter stopped and faced him.

"I'm really sorry, I'm not feeling very well." He pointed to the wound. "This was my retirement gift from one of my customers and it's itching like mad."

"It's gone bad, Jim. You need to see a doctor."

"I will. Which house belongs to Willis?"

The question clearly caught Peter off guard, more so than Stokes's earlier use of colourful language. He frowned, showing deep trenches in his forehead. Stokes had never seen them before on Peter's usually jolly expression.

"Willis? Why?"

It was obvious Peter had little time for Willis and he didn't care if he showed it.

"He said something about the house to me the other day and I'd like to ask him what he meant. He wasn't at the last meeting so…"

"What did he say?"

"Nothing really, he just hinted at something."

Peter looked over Stokes's shoulder at the cottage. "I didn't want to say anything before but he's crackers. He was in an institution a couple of years back, lost his house and everything. I'd leave him well enough alone if I were you."

Stokes felt the desire to grab Peter around the neck and shake him until his teeth rattled together.

"I'd like to speak to him, Peter," he said flatly.

"You won't get much sense out of him, but if you want to waste some of your time then that's your choice. He lives two doors down from the hall. You can't miss it, it looks like a house a lunatic might live in."

"Thanks." He turned to walk away but felt Peter's hand on his shoulder.

"Jim, you look terrible and it's not man-flu. You need to see a doctor."

Stokes half-turned and smiled. "I will."

He walked quickly back to the cottage and without turning, knew Peter was watching him. He could watch all he liked.

Stokes looked across the lake and for a moment he was tempted to hurl himself into the water and swim to the other side. He'd never felt better than he did right now. The rain had washed his troubles away, just like he knew they would. How far could it be? A mile, two at the most. He hadn't done any swimming for years but just to immerse himself in the water would feel like heaven. He paused before going back inside and shivered violently. The wound seeped blood, so pale and diluted by the rain, that it looked vaguely like fruit juice. In a way it was – extract from a crushed man.

He examined his reflection in the glass. He looked old

and haggard. He looked the same as the street drinkers looked after a couple of years on the old White Lightning cider. He'd never been fat but could've done with losing a couple of pounds, yet now he looked lean. He put his hands into the small of his back and stretched. The hole in his torso opened up where his body was attempting to heal. He didn't want it to heal over again, he would never allow it. It was a little keepsake. He dug his hand into his pocket and pulled out the teeth. They were a keepsake too.

He pushed a tooth into the open wound, then another and another until all five were gone. He stepped inside. There were another fifteen to go and they were small enough to fit inside perfectly. If it was a bit tight in there, well he might just have to make their new home a little bigger.

*

He sat on the hatch and spread the remaining hair and teeth out in front of him. The little girl had put them in a safe place when she'd hidden them, inside the box, but it seemed right that they should be out in the daylight again. Why on earth would she hide them anyway?

Perhaps she hadn't. Lots of people kept trinkets to remember their children's younger years. Maybe her mum and dad had put them there for safekeeping and simply forgotten them when they moved on.

He pulled a few strands of hair to his nose and inhaled. How was it they smelled so fresh? He closed his eyes and imagined her standing before him. Her front two teeth would be missing and she'd poke her tongue through the gap at him. They'd both laugh and he'd chase her around the house until they collapsed breathless and giggling.

"Daddy?"

His eyes flicked open.

"Daddy? Am I beautiful?" There she was, standing before him just as he'd imagined it.

"You are the most beautiful girl in the world."

This time there was no hint of a smile, it was a great beaming grin and it covered most of her face. Daylight wormed its way through the glass doors. It fell on the room, it fell on her, but mostly it fell through her and changed from a grim and grey late-autumn afternoon sun into a mid-summer haze. It was bewitching.

"What's your name?" he asked.

"Melody," she answered immediately.

"What a pretty name. Do you live here?"

The smile left her face and was replaced with a pained expression. "No, a nasty man brought me here." Her voice was little more than a whisper.

Stokes didn't know what to say. He was well used to having conversations with the ghosts his mind conjured up, but those conversations had usually consisted of vitriolic threats of violence. This was entirely different.

"We have something in common then." He looked down at the scar. One of the teeth protruded slightly so he pushed it gently back inside.

"I know you're not really here, Melody. I've not been quite right for a while, not since... not since a nasty woman did something to me. She took me somewhere I didn't want to go and she left me there." He paused and looked at her again. She simply stared at him. "I think I might still be there actually and I can't seem to find my way back. If there is a way back anymore."

"Help?" she whispered.

"Help?" he whispered back. Which one of them was asking for help? Both of them?

She looked down at the teeth, firstly at the collection by his feet then, tipping her head to one side, at the ones in his wound.

"I'm keeping them safe. Are they yours?"

The light continued to fall against her tiny frame, but instead of her body turning it into a summer haze, she became a hellish prism and turned the sunlight into a storm cloud which landed like a dirty puddle at her feet.

She opened her mouth and Stokes instinctively raised his hands to cover his ears. For all the world she looked as if she were about to scream. Instead, blood dripped slowly from her gums. She had not a single tooth in her head and as she closed her mouth again, her face became twisted.

"Am I beautiful, Daddy?" Her words were almost unrecognisable.

But she was beautiful. She could never be anything other than perfect.

"Of course, but I'm not your daddy."

"Daddy? Help?"

He remembered hearing a voice like that once before, in a different world. It was a time when things had been more ordered and easy to understand. It was a long time before Natalie Sutton had got her hands on him. He'd been a uniformed police officer then and when someone asked for help you gave it. And when that someone was a little lost girl, you did everything you could to help, and then you did some more.

"I'll help you." He nodded. "I'm going to help you, Melody."

*

The light had slipped away some time ago but Stokes waited on the floor with his collection. He was waiting for her to return, he was waiting for her to come back and call him Daddy again. He took his eyes away from the hatch and looked out onto the lake. They took a few seconds to focus; it had been a few hours since they had looked at anything other than a square of wooden floor.

Someone had started a bonfire on the far side of the lake and orange embers leapt haphazardly into the air. He inhaled deeply and caught the faint scent of the fire. A spark flew higher than the others and exploded suddenly in a fizzing shower of multi-coloured stars. Was it November the fifth already? The bang of the firework reached him. It couldn't possibly be November already because that would mean he'd been in the cottage for what..? Weeks? Or was it months? Had he always been here?

He felt tired again. The only time he'd ever felt like this was after the night-shifts on a Saturday night; after being run ragged by revellers enjoying their weekend by trying to beat each other's brains in. He dragged himself upright and clutched the trinkets tightly to his chest. The blackness from the wound was creeping slowly upward and across his body. It was level with the bottom of his ribcage now but what would happen once it reached his face? Would it simply stop or would it slither into his head via his nose or his ears? He trailed his finger over the dark and shiny skin. If it managed to get into his head, good luck to it. There were worse things than a bit of necrosis in there, oh yes, a lot worse.

He staggered upstairs and climbed onto the dirty bed. What had Willis actually said about the cottage? He'd asked if he knew anything about the cottage or something like that.

"No, I don't," he answered.

But now he should know something about it, shouldn't he? Now he had a little girl to look after.

He shuffled about on the bed but it wasn't comfortable. Why was he up here anyway? She'd asked him for help and he couldn't do that if they weren't together.

Scretch, scretch, scretch.

"I'm coming, Melody." He swung his legs off the side of the bed. "I'm on my way."

He padded back downstairs and lifted the hatch. "Daddy's here."

Some of the teeth were tangled up with hair again and he pushed two more inside the wound. He clutched the others in his fist. The pain took his breath away momentarily and a wave of nausea and vertigo almost dropped him into the hole head-first. He clamped his teeth together as hard as he could and felt the enamel grind away.

He dropped into the hole and pulled the hatch over his head. He felt calm and relaxed now he was back down here.

Scretch, scretch, scretch.

The poor girl had lost all of her teeth but that didn't make her appear any less beautiful. Perhaps it would make her feel a little better if he didn't have any teeth either? He could show her that she was wonderful, just as she was, with or without teeth.

He tugged on his front two teeth. They wouldn't come out without a fight but maybe it was a battle he ought to take.

"Where are you?"

"I'm here, Daddy," a voice whispered in the darkness. Her voice, although faint, seemed to come from all around him.

"I can't see you." He turned in a circle.

"Just here."

He felt a cold hand take his own. It was so small and delicate that as he gripped it, he felt he might squeeze too hard and shatter her fragile little bones.

"You look tired, Daddy. You should come and lie down."

He felt his feet start to move but he didn't feel in

control of them.

"Just over here."

She led him into a dark corner and let go of his hand.

"I'll sleep just here and you can sleep just there if you like?"

Stokes nodded and smiled. He could see nothing.

"That way, if I get frightened I'll know you're right next to me and I won't be scared anymore."

"Of course, I'll always be here, Melody. There's no need to be frightened anymore."

They both dropped down and lay back. The earth under his body didn't feel damp or unyielding, quite the contrary, it felt as warm and comfortable as any bed he'd ever put his head on. As he started to drift off to sleep he felt Melody's icy-cold body push against his own.

"It's nice down here, isn't it, Daddy?"

Stokes nodded, he was unable to speak.

"Other people might like it too, don't you think?"

And she was right. An enormous sense of happiness washed over him. He didn't want to share this feeling with anyone, not ever, it should always be just like this.

"Lots of other people." There was a strange tone to her voice, but he was too tired and too damned happy for a change to think about it.

"Other people," he murmured and fell asleep.

12

Edward Willis stood in his kitchen and looked out over the lake. One day soon a reckoning was coming and he was ready for it. He was ready to meet whoever was in charge of the next place and kick them in the balls. Life was shit and it was all their fault. Had it always been a stinking turd? Mostly yes, but it got worse after life threw him into that parish. Then life really started to reek. They'd wanted help from him when he could barely help himself. He slumped into the chair and put the TV on. Soap operas, bloody soap operas all night. He threw his empty coffee mug at the screen but it missed and shattered against the wall. Before they'd darkened his doorstep he was just another vicar waiting for his pension. Now look what they'd made him do. Christ, he was angry. He couldn't remember a time when he wasn't angry, when he wasn't tired and angry and he was getting to the end of his tether with it, with thinking about them. He closed his eyes and tried to remember the way things were but the scene played itself out the same each and every time.

*

"She's our daughter, for Christ's sake! Can you hear yourself? Do you know what you're saying?"

Willis nodded. The couple had come to him for help with their daughter. They had put faith in him and in God to help them and the girl. He was desperately out of his depth and not just because the girl was so obviously troubled, but because he wasn't who they thought he was.

"I can understand your reluctance but…"

The man held up his hand. "No buts, this is just… medieval and I won't have it." He looked at his wife and stood up.

This was the woman Willis had been sleeping with for the last six months. They'd come to him for help and he'd seduced her and then fucked her in their bed while hubby was at work.

Now she looked to him for guidance when he was as troubled as the girl.

"I can help her, you just have to trust me." Trust him? Ha! That was a joke. He was about as trustworthy as Lucifer. Nevertheless, he was a good liar and when he spoke with conviction like he just had, people listened. God only knew why but they did.

"We should trust him. I trust him." The wife looked at them each in turn. She wasn't exactly attractive and he'd had better in the last parish, but there was something about her wholesome village nature that appealed to him. She hadn't exactly been unwilling, had she? No, she'd been active to the point of domination.

The man stopped in stunned silence and looked at his wife. "Why? Why should we trust him? There are other doctors, there are other…"

"No, there aren't. Did you see what she did to the other children in the playground?"

He stayed silent and looked at the floor.

"I was there picking up the pieces, literally. *'They've got nasty words written on their faces, Mummy, and they're all about me. I tried to rub them out but I couldn't do it, not without the rock.'* And she smiled at me with the bloody rock in one hand as if it was the most natural thing in the world."

"But she's just a little girl, she's our little Melody."

He watched as the father fell back onto the sofa. He was a pathetic figure, the typical cuckold in many ways.

The wife continued, "I know you're frightened of her, I know you are. You can't even look at her anymore, neither of us can. One day she'll see something plastered all over our faces and it'll be something she doesn't like. What if she decides to rub it out with a knife or boiling water?"

The man snivelled and held his hands up to his face.

"We do this on our terms or the authorities will do it for us. She goes with Edward tonight to the lake. We tell them she's run away from home and we carry on like we've lost her."

"And then what?" He was angry. "We just miraculously find her and everyone's happy? It won't work like that."

"We disappear. We all do." Willis spoke quietly but assuredly. This was what God wanted from him, wasn't it? To help people in their darkest hours, when all else had failed and they didn't know where to turn next.

Did he really believe that?

Not so long ago there was a time when he felt those things, not just heard them, but felt them deep down in the pit of his stomach. Those feelings were so strong that they almost knocked the wind out of him. That was God's call but he couldn't remember the last time he'd heard it.

The man turned to him now. "And aren't you afraid she'll try and do the same to you, Willis? She knows things about you too, she's seen them. Your profession doesn't give you immunity."

He touched the dog-collar around his neck. "She won't be seeing anything or anyone for a while, not even me."

"Oh God!" The father threw his head back.

Willis exchanged a look with the woman.

"Yes, it is God who will help Melody," he said. Was this a test? Was this the latest in a long line of examinations, all of which he seemed to be failing miserably? He couldn't help thinking about the wife's breasts; those big bouncing breasts with beautiful, pink nipples.

He knelt beside the weeping man and put his hand on his wife's naked knee. "You must trust me and you must trust God. We will never turn our back on you or Melody."

This was his chance of salvation. This was his last

chance to do something other than lie to people. He would save the girl and in doing so he would save himself.

He showed them out and closed the door behind them. He slid down the door and sat on the floor. "Am I doing the right thing?" He thumped the back of his head against the door.

"Answer me. Just this once, answer me."

Medically, the girl had been examined and she was as perfect as her parents wanted her to be. Psychosis, that was the diagnosis, but what did that really mean? Spiritually, that was where the troubles were and the only person who knew how to truly diagnose that had been dead for over two thousand years.

She was haunted by hallucinations of a kind that were alarming and disturbing to others, yet to her they were perfectly natural. The parents had tried everything but the aberrations remained and were seemingly there to stay. The episode with the other children in the playground was startling but the incident in the church was a far more distressing event. She'd spoken to him at the foot of the pulpit and as he'd looked into her vivid blue eyes, he'd seen the words reflected onto his own – 'faithless' and 'adulterer'. He'd wiped his head so that the congregation couldn't see them, so they couldn't see his own failings. She had missed one though, one that was worse than anything else he could imagine.

'Suicide'.

Every time he looked in the mirror, he saw it etched upon his own face.

"Am I doing the right thing?" That was the question he'd asked as he swallowed the last tablet all those years ago.

He'd take her up to the lake house. This was the cottage where he'd grown up, where his own mother and father had given him almost everything he'd desired. Almost but not quite.

His father had tried to seduce almost every woman in the village at one time or another and his mother had been too drunk to notice. The constant arguments and the never-ending late night parties had kept him awake throughout most of his childhood, yet the gifts made up for it. A steady stream of the latest toys and gadgets had been a welcome diversion from the maelstrom around him.

So why had he chosen the church? Or rather, why had the church chosen him?

He'd not so much heard the word of God but felt it. Deep, deep down in his guts, amid the whirling cacophony that was a typical night in the Willis house, he'd felt it. As sure as can be, he'd felt it. It hit him so hard that he fell, panting and winded from his little bed. It didn't feel odd or strange to him though, it felt right and it was a way out of the house. It was something to aim for.

He pulled himself upright and walked into the front room. Her perfume still hung in the air and it aroused him. Her impatient fingers at his zip, her hot breath on his torso and...

"Edward? Have they gone?"

"Yes," he called up the stairs.

"Are you coming up to play then?"

He smirked and touched the dog-collar.

"Leave the collar on, please. I like it on."

He jogged up the stairs. It was probably a good idea to leave town for a while anyway. Sleeping with the daughter of another prominent member of the congregation was bound to get out sooner or later.

"On my way."

*

Willis bit his lip hard enough to draw blood. He'd kept that little girl locked up for so long she'd become something else, she'd become a demon and it was all their fault. They'd made him do it.

They wanted everything to be perfect. They wanted their world to be filled with sugar plum fairies and little girls in gingham dresses, and if something didn't fit into that scheme, well it was just discarded like waste.

Yet he had been complicit, there was no denying that. The duplicity of his own wretched soul was a disgrace. With one hand he would offer help, pleading for the opportunity to aid those who suffered, and yet with the other he would search out an opening to suit his own ends, to aid with his own redemption. He had sought this above all else. He had conspired with his own madness until lunacy prevailed and led him down a path which was awash with the blood of a little girl. And for what? For forgiveness? From whom?

From a God who had never even tried to converse with him, not even when he was on the brink. He licked at the blood on his lips. Physically, he was intact but beneath his worn and leathery skin lived a soul which was forever damaged. A soul which deserved to be torn into a thousand pieces, put back together and torn asunder again and again and again for all eternity.

Was there a chance for redemption?

He didn't want it. He had forfeited that shot when he allowed his own pride to stop what he knew was wrong. What had they been thinking? What had any of them been thinking? Were they all so damaged that their vision was blinded by blackened and disease-ridden cataracts? Yet even through the fogged vision they should have seen her for what she was – a sweet and frightened little girl who did not deserve to see out her days in a pit.

Willis groaned and raised his hands to his face. If he had the strength he would do what he had tried to do before, twice.

He threw back his head and shouted with as much force as he was able. "Forgive me Melody, forgive me!"

He slumped forward and allowed a child-like whimper to escape him. There may be no chance of redemption, there should be none, but he could no longer stand the abject sound of his own thoughts. He must do something, not for himself but for the girl. It must be for the girl and only for her.

He gathered himself together and climbed the stairs to his bedroom. Judging by what he'd seen a few nights ago, the man Stokes was deranged, and capable of almost anything. He pulled open the drawer containing his underwear and socks and slid his hand toward the back. His fingers touched the cold metal of the key to the cottage as they had done a hundred times. He pulled it out and examined the indentations on the metal. It was as unremarkable as it was poignant. This would be the last time he held the key between his fingers, he was sure of that.

He looked out of the window and watched as the familiar pattern of lights from the houses across Stormark were fanned by the bowing trees. It was early evening but night, true night, was still so far away. Stokes was clearly a night-owl, but surely even he slept some nights. The man had seemed so normal when they'd met. He didn't listen to the idle tattle of the villagers very often but he'd heard them whispering about the ex-copper coming to live in the cottage. It had been a shock and, at first, a source of anxiety and worry, but as he had come to this final resolution it no longer mattered. Perhaps he too was haunted by the ghosts of badly made decisions and they stopped him from sleeping. Perhaps everyone shared those demons which came hurtling into your head at three in the morning.

He wiped the blood from his lips. Not everyone possessed the dark and guilty soul of a habitual insomniac. Not everyone claimed to be a man of God and had murdered a little girl.

He sat on the bed and stared at the key. "Am I doing

the right thing?"

The wind screamed down the chimney and blew the kitchen door shut. It rattled against its hinges and fell silent.

Willis laughed. "Is that a yes?"

13

She was a monster, she knew that now. If it had been her own parents, which she thought it probably was, they had screamed when they saw her. And if she was a monster then it was their fault, not all their fault because the Vicar was to blame too but mostly their fault.

Had she been a monster before they locked her away though? She ran her hands over her head. It was completely bald now and it felt creepy. She could even feel where parts of her skull were knitted together. She shivered and chuckled to herself. The Vicar had brought them here, to look at her, but why? They hadn't spoken and the light from the sun was too bright to see if they had any words written across their faces. She wouldn't have liked to see their faces though, not really. The words wouldn't have been nice ones, they would've probably been like those girls at school – mean and nasty.

The Vicar didn't seem nasty, at least not like a proper nasty man. He brought her food and came to speak to her sometimes but she couldn't work him out, not without seeing his face. She might like to see that, at least for a little while.

Footsteps overhead. That usually meant he was on his way down to see her. She smiled and scuttled off into the darkest corner she knew. It was where she went to the toilet and not even the rats went there.

A shaft of light shot down in a perfect square and lit up the floor. It looked like the light looked inside a church, when the sun shone through one of the big windows. If he just turned around once she might see him and understand him a little better.

"Melody?" He always tried to sound friendly but it didn't work. There was a hint of annoyance in his tone, like when a teacher was impatient.

She crouched a little lower and watched him drop into the cellar.

"Are you there, Melody? I've got some sandwiches for you."

She could see the plate in his hand but as he pulled the hatch back over he was just a shape, just like always. Everything was a shape now, a dark shape. The rats were just scurrying little shapes which sometimes possessed shiny black gems if a fragment of light touched them. The Vicar was just a featureless shape which shuffled slowly and awkwardly around the cellar. If she had never seen him, never seen a human being, she might think he was a shambling beast from one of the story books in her room.

In her room?

Wasn't this her room?

"Melody, come to me, please. Come and have something to eat."

She hissed back at him. She'd heard the rats do it to each other, especially when they were about to fight and bite each other. Her effort didn't sound as good as the rats and it made a wet noise but she was pleased with the result. The Vicar turned in a circle to face her direction but she could tell by the way he quickly moved his head from side to side that he couldn't see her.

"I can see you," she whispered and scurried to the other side of the cellar.

"Melody, now is not the time for silly games. Come and get your dinner."

He hadn't taken a step in any direction yet but he swivelled on his toes, searching in the darkness for her.

"Was that my mum and dad?" she whispered and went on the move again.

She watched him turn to the last place she'd been in. "Your parents were here, yes. They came to see how you were getting along. They wanted to see if you were ready to go home."

She felt a heaviness in her tummy and it made her want to cry. She swallowed it back, the way she'd done when she'd first seen Daddy's face after the incident at church.

"Why did Mummy scream?" She didn't move this time.

The Vicar turned again and this time he looked directly into her eyes. "She was frightened, Melody."

"Frightened of me?"

The Vicar edged forward. "If you come and eat your dinner we can talk about it properly."

"I'm not hungry." She really wasn't either.

He took another step forward. "You must be, you haven't eaten anything for four days. Come on Melody, this isn't funny now."

She ran toward him, shoved him as she ducked under his outstretched arm. "I said I'm not hungry." She was past him and hidden by the darkness again before he'd even had time to turn. This was fun.

"I'm going to leave your food for the rats then," he shouted.

She watched him tip the plate, allowing the sandwiches to fall to the floor. She didn't mind, she didn't expect to feel hungry again, ever.

He turned and took a step toward where the hatch was.

"What don't you believe in anymore?"

He stopped dead.

"You had the word 'faithless' written across your face in the church. There were other words too but some of them flashed too quickly and I couldn't read them. 'Faithless' and 'adulterer' were the clearest and the brightest."

He span around quickly. His face was bright red but not with words, with anger and it painted the walls of the cellar a deep red.

"It means I fucked your dear mummy, Melody. I fucked her and we both loved it."

She hissed at him and then laughed. "Oh I know that, I've seen it on both of your faces. Daddy knows too. Why are you faithless?"

"I'm not!" he almost barked.

"You are, I saw it. Just the same as I knew the doctor liked to touch his niece, just the same as I knew the other children in the playground hated me. It was written all over them. Is it God?"

He took a step toward her. "Come here, Melody."

She backed away. He sounded angry, really angry. "Is God down here with me?" she asked.

He took another step.

"I wonder what God has got written on his face?"

"Shut up!"

She sat down, beside the rats' nest and slipped her hand inside the warm hole. "I don't think he'd have anything there because he isn't real. Is that what you think too?"

"You better be quiet or…"

"Or what, you'll send me to see for myself?" She dragged a baby rat from the hole. It squeaked at her and tried to wriggle free.

"Oh, I might just do that."

She jumped up and threw the baby rat at the dark shape she knew was his head. It wobbled through the air and hit him. She giggled and started to run toward the other side.

"You'll have to catch me first!"

He lurched forward and made a lunge for her but she

was too quick and avoided him easily.

"Come here!" he roared.

She laughed and picked up a lump of damp earth. "You're too slow." She hurled the mud at him and saw the black star-burst as it hit him.

He lumbered toward her, a great hulking monster from the shadows.

"Why don't you believe in him? Is it my mum's fault, did she make you stop?"

"I do believe, I do. Stop it!"

"Why? Would you let me leave if I did?"

He stopped. "I might."

She laughed and scooped up some more dirt, this handful had spiky stones in too. She hurled them and ran back toward the rats.

"I don't want to leave. I like it here, I want to stay." She was giggling. This was like a game she used to play with the other children. Was it called Tag?

"Then you'll die and it'll be soon."

"I know I will, it's written in big letters all over me. I can feel them scratching away at me, from the inside."

She sat beside the rats' nest again. The nest was like a factory, it just kept producing more and more babies, more and more and more. She plunged her hand inside again and pulled one free. It was a little older than the others and it hissed at her. It was angry and if she loosened her hold on its neck just a bit, it would bite her, they'd done it before.

She squeezed its throat just a little bit but hard enough

to make those beautiful gems bulge. She knew what would happen if she squeezed too hard – those jewels would just pop right out and land on the filthy ground. She moved her head closer, close enough so the rat's whiskers brushed the end of her nose. Those deep dark eyes were like bottomless ponds of ink. She could stare at them for hours and never was there anything but darkness; no red-flashing neon with spidery words written in them. They were perfect.

"Perfect," she whispered.

She brought the rat a little closer. That was strange, there was something written in them this time. It was faint but it was creeping closer, rising to the surface of the pond. She couldn't make it out but there were words, lots of them and all of them had spiky little tails trailing from the letters.

Closer and closer.

"Fear," she whispered and turned around.

The monster vicar loomed above her and in his eyes a thousand words flashed in an instant. They were so bright they stung her eyes.

"Will you kill me now?" she asked. It was in his eyes, not written, but there for all to see.

The cellar was awash with red and it dripped from the walls like blood pouring from a deep cut.

"I can't help you." His voice sounded sad but not shaky like it did when people were crying.

She felt his hands around her throat. His thumbs pushed against her windpipe and his forefingers dug painfully into her jaw. She tried to keep her feet on the ground but she felt him lifting her upward until she couldn't even reach with her tip-toes. She stared into his eyes and the words kept spinning like a crazy fruit machine. Over and over again the same words appeared and in the same order. Fear, hate, suicide, faithless and dead.

Were they his words or were they a reflection of the words painted across her own face? Was she seeing what he was seeing? Were they seeing the same thing?

"Am I doing the right thing?" She saw his mouth move and yet the words seemed to come from another place, from another person in another time. His mouth was an ugly snarl and a froth gathered at the corners where his top and bottom lips met. It wouldn't have surprised her to see a vile little insect crawl out from the foam just like it did with cuckoo-spit.

The room grew darker now, even though the words burned brighter still in his eyes. Darker and darker. Darker and darker.

Dead. That was the brightest word. That had always been the brightest word.

14

Stokes awoke with a start. Where was he?

Ah yes, he was in bed, in his new and comfortable bed down in the cellar. He groaned. It was the pain that had awakened him. It seemed his whole body now trembled in fear at each passing beat of his heart. Make this the last one, please. *One last pump of that good old Stokes blood around the hectic helter-skelter track and then be still.*

In the last three days, he'd only stepped out of the hole on one occasion and that was to fetch his hammer. He ran his tongue across the jagged tombstones he'd made of his teeth. His upper lip felt swollen and grotesque. The first blow from the hammer had been far too tentative and his lips had rolled over the teeth in some pathetic protective gesture. Somewhere deep down, his body wanted to help him scramble back out of the pit. Too little too late. The steel smashed into the lip and the incisors. The pain had been staggering but as he choked back blood, his own metallic blood, he smashed the hammer into his teeth again.

Melody had helped him through it. She'd held his hand and urged him on when he could barely hold the hammer's wooden handle for all the blood. She'd whispered to him and told him how much it would mean to her if both of them looked the same; if neither of them had teeth anymore. That way nobody would ever doubt they were father and daughter. She was right.

He looked down at her and smiled. Addicts with blackened and missing teeth from all the sugary methadone they took had better smiles than him. They probably felt better than him too.

She sat up and hugged him, and for a moment the pain vanished into the darkness.

"There's someone here, Daddy," she whispered into his ear sending a shiver through his body.

"Where?" He eased her away from him so he could see her.

She put a finger to her lips and pointed to the floorboards above their heads.

Stokes looked up, dazed and confused. He opened his mouth to speak but stopped instantly at the sound of creaking… the sound of footsteps.

His eyes widened. Someone else was in the house. Was it Natalie? Had she come back to ruin his life again? He followed the footsteps above until they stopped on the hatch.

"We have to move." He spoke in a whisper but it sounded like a bark. "Come on, we have to…"

He turned to where Melody had been just a moment before, but she wasn't there.

"Melody," he whispered as loud as he dared and scampered across the dirt away from the hatch.

A hazy shaft of light pierced the darkness and created jagged patterns in the dank air as the hatch lifted slowly open. He was transfixed by it. It reminded him of how Natalie's blade must have ignited in the afternoon sun just before it ripped into his flesh.

"Natalie…"

But it wasn't Natalie who descended into the cellar. It was much too large to be her, much too bulky for someone on the H-plan diet. Whoever it was pulled the hatch back over their hooded head and in doing so, gave themselves the gift of disguise.

He looked around. Where was Melody? Things felt confused, in fact they'd pretty much gone to rat shit, but he had to keep her safe. He knew that much. That was his purpose now.

The man, because it had to be a man from the sheer size, had a torch and he flicked it around the darkness like a lightsaber. But he didn't do it in a random sweep, he shone the torch quickly but without care or pause before he settled on his direction.

He was shuffling slowly but definitely toward the spot where Stokes had just come from, where not two minutes before he'd been sleeping as soundly as he had in months.

"He's come to take me away," Melody again whispered in his ear. It was almost as if she'd been inside his head and seen the question forming in his brain.

He bit down on his bottom lip as pain erupted in his gut. It was all he could do to stop himself from crying out.

The other man stopped and flashed the torch in their direction. The beam of light hit Stokes and travelled right through his flesh, burning his nerves as it went. How could he not have seen them? Either of them.

"Stay still." He turned to Melody but she'd gone again.

The torchlight whipped back across the room and wobbled away again. Why would they have come to take Melody away? It didn't make any sense. Worse still, it frightened him. Nobody had the right to take her away... to take her away from him. If they took her then what would he have left? Nothing except an old house, a poisoned body and a ruined mind. No, nobody was taking her away from him or this house, not now, not ever.

He pushed himself down into the dirt and slithered across the mud like a snake.

Stokes's eyes had adjusted to the blackness but even so the man was nothing more than a dark shape, hulking and distorted. The intruder dropped the torch to the ground and lowered himself slowly to his knees. This was an older man who suffered with his joints, or his back, or maybe both. He hunched over and began frantically scratching at the earth.

Stokes watched intently. This was almost the exact spot where he'd been lying, he was positive. He crawled closer. The man grunted as he sunk his hands into the ground but he worked with a frenzied pace as he threw the earth to one side. He was like a deranged treasure hunter. Deeper and deeper he dug until the grunts slowly turned into a pathetic whimper. Was he disappointed by his lack of success?

"He's found me."

He didn't turn this time – he could see Melody was already in the man's arms. He cradled her with a tenderness Stokes had only seen before from new fathers on a maternity ward. The same fathers who had beaten their pregnant wives to within an inch of their miserable lives only a week before and it was sickening. He could see Melody clearly, her light and fragile frame sinking into the monster's arms as if she were nothing more than a bundle of twigs. It was heartbreaking. She looked toward him but she said nothing. She didn't need to. The word written across her poor face was clear enough. It was scrawled in the same colour as the blood which Natalie had extracted from him and it was too much to see.

Dead.

He scrambled to his feet. "Leave her alone, you bastard!" His tongue and lips were swollen and the words scraped against the shards his teeth had become on their way out of his mouth.

The other man turned and even in the darkness, Stokes saw the whites of his eyes. He dropped Melody instantly and she fell to the earth without a sound.

"You just leave her alone or I'll kill you." He clenched his fists and felt the adrenalin surge through his body. It sent a horrible spasm through his gut but his mind pushed it aside. Now was not the time to double over, now was the time to fight.

"Mr Stokes? Is that you?"

He recognised the voice but the echo made it sound like a demon speaking in tongues. He took a step forward.

"Mr Stokes, I'm sorry, I'm not sure I know…"

"You shouldn't have come here, you won't take Melody."

The other man took a step back. "Melody?" His voice trembled. "You know… How…?"

Stokes stepped forward again. He knew the voice from somewhere, he'd spoken with its owner before.

"She's staying with me. I won't let you take her."

The other man started snivelling but Stokes felt nothing except a fierce sense of protection.

"He's a nasty man, Daddy. Don't let him touch me again."

"I won't let him, sweetheart. Don't worry."

"Mr Stokes, Jim? It's me, Edward Willis, from the village." He was crying properly now.

A flash of the man walking along the lane in the rain flashed across Stokes's memory. He was a miserable man, a dejected man.

"Willis," he murmured.

"Who are you talking to?" Panic had started to splash through his tears now and his voice lifted an octave.

"Melody." Stokes reached Willis. They stood toe to toe and Stokes could see him clearly now. His coat gave him a false stature. He was nothing but a feeble old man.

"Look at her, you've scared her." He pointed at the floor where there was now a hole.

Willis looked down where he was pointing. "Bones, it's nothing but bones, Mr Stokes." He dropped to his knees and wailed. "I put her there." He lifted his head and shouted, "I put her there! Did you hear me? I put her there!"

Stokes looked at Melody. "Bones? That's a beautiful little girl. Don't you dare speak to her like that."

"I'm frightened of him," Melody whispered.

Stokes raised his fist and brought it down on Willis's nose. He heard a terrible crack as the blow sent the old man to the earth.

"You won't touch her again," he snarled and raised his fist once more. Willis looked up at him and in that brief moment, Stokes saw his own reflection in the other man's eyes. He was a skeletal horror with the word 'dead' painted in big red letters across his forehead. He smashed his fist into Willis's face again and felt warm blood splash across his cheek. He raised his fist again. Nobody was going to take her away. Nobody.

"Kill him, send him down!" There was something about Melody's voice, something he didn't like and it brought him back from the brink.

"I can't," he muttered and looked down at Willis, then at his own hand. He uncurled his fist and felt a sticky resistance. How many times had he struck the man? Once? Twice? He couldn't be sure. He wasn't sure of anything anymore.

He reached down and tried to pull Willis upright but the man was a deadweight. He was out cold and judging by the distorted mass of flesh across the front of his face, his nose was now in several pieces.

"You shouldn't have come here. You shouldn't have touched her." He grabbed Willis under the armpits and dragged him into the corner, away from the little hole he'd been digging. What would he do with him? Willis had broken in and attempted to... attempted to do what? Dig a hole? Whatever his intention it was still burglary and that meant he should call the local boys in blue, wherever they were stationed.

"We could have a party?" Melody appeared beside Willis in the corner. She stroked his head. "If we had a few more people, that is."

"What?"

"There were others too."

"Others? What do you mean?"

"This man killed me, Daddy. He killed me and do you know what he was?"

Stokes shook his head.

"He was an adulterer and he didn't believe in God. He was a vicar, you know. He was other things too but I couldn't see the other things quite so clearly."

Stokes looked at them both. Willis's head lolled over to one side with a dark stream of blood running from where his nose was. Melody wiggled her fingers in it as if it was a cool mountain stream.

"Mummy was an adulterer too, you know that don't

you, Daddy? She was an adulterer with the Vicar."

Stokes opened his mouth to speak, to tell her he wasn't her real daddy and that her daddy would be along soon to collect her and take her away.

Take her away.

"Did he keep you down here?"

She nodded.

"Did your mummy know?"

She nodded again.

"Why?" He took a step toward her.

"Because she couldn't see the words like I could. Nobody could, not even the other girls at school, and it scared them. I think, I scared them. None of them would look at me anymore."

Stokes knelt in front of her. "I want to look at you."

"I know you do. You see the words too sometimes, don't you?"

He nodded.

She beamed back at him and in that moment all of her perfect little teeth reflected what little light there was. They shone in the darkness like the little gems they were. Then they were gone again.

He looked at Willis and grimaced. "And this man kept you down here until all those beautiful teeth fell out, didn't he?"

He reached down and pulled one free from his torso. He traced his finger over the jagged edge before pushing it into Willis's forehead. It made a crude but effective blade.

"Now I'll make sure everyone can see what's written on

his forehead."

Slowly he scratched the word killer into Willis's furrowed and bloody brow.

Melody giggled in his ear. She giggled like the little girl she was; like the little girl she had never been allowed to be.

He got to his feet and crouched over Willis. "How long were you down here?"

She looked up at him. "I don't know. I think it was a long time though."

"I think the Vicar should stay down here a very long time too." He shuffled toward the hatch.

"Don't leave me," she whimpered.

He turned and smiled. "I'll be right back, just watch him. I want to make sure he can't leave."

He resumed toward the hatch. He'd once found a man whose feet had been smashed to pieces over a drug feud. They'd been pounded with a lump hammer and chisel until they were nothing more than a tangled mass of splintered bones. The victim would never be able to walk again, let alone peddle his drugs through the city.

Now, where had he left his tools?

*

He dragged everything out of cupboards and even checked under the bed but he couldn't find what he was looking for. There were spanners, screwdrivers and even an old rusty hacksaw, but no hammer. He had one, of course he did, but where was it? He stopped and scratched at the gaping hole in his gut. God, it itched. He wanted to stick his fingers inside and just give it a good old poke. Those little teeth in there helped but it was on the verge of driving him… what? Mad?

Was he there already? If he was asking the question then that was a good sign, it had to be. His whole body felt prickly, as if he'd just walked naked through a meadow full of nettles. It was difficult to see where his skin ended and the dirt began now. There was probably a good mix of blood in there too, blood and pus.

Was this real? Was any of it actually real?

Was Natalie real? Was Edward Willis really slumped in the cellar being watched over by a little, lost girl?

Was he really contemplating hobbling the man?

"Too many questions." He rubbed at his temples with the heels of his hands. It didn't matter if none of it was real, did it?

"Under the bed," he whispered to himself and rushed upstairs. The toolbox, his good toolbox was under the bed.

"Jim?"

He heard the female voice but it didn't register. It wasn't as important as finding the toolbox and the lump hammer. The lighter claw hammer had been fine for DIY dentistry but he had no idea where that was. Besides, the lump hammer had a real heft to it, just right for breaking bones.

"Jim, are you there?"

There it was again.

"Go away," he shouted. "Leave me alone, I'm busy."

And he was. He was about to break every fragile bone in Edward Willis's ankles.

"Jim, it's us." This time it was a man's voice.

"I said I'm busy!" He pulled the hammer out and spun it in the air. It landed perfectly in his hand. He smiled and ran down the stairs.

"Jim? What are you doing?"

Stokes was taken aback. Sure, he'd heard voices but they were somewhere else, someplace else. Now there were two people standing on the threshold to his cottage. He stared at them in the gloom.

"Jim, it's me, Ina."

Stokes stared at them. He knew Ina and Peter but were they really there?

"I told you, he needs to go to the hospital." He saw Peter's hand reach out and touch his wife's shoulder.

Ina crouched and placed the cake tin she had been holding on the boards. Stokes smiled. If the cake was heavy enough it might just go right through the boards and land on Willis's head. That would save him some trouble.

He tossed the hammer into the air and caught it. "What can I do for you?"

Neither of them made any effort to step inside the house. "Peter mentioned he'd seen you yesterday and you were…"

"I was what? Rude? Yes I was and I apologised." He turned to Peter. "Didn't I?" He knew he sounded aggressive. He didn't care, he wanted to be.

"No, not rude, Jim, just odd."

"Odd? Probably. Things have been a bit strange…" He paused and looked at them each in turn. "Sorry, what do you want?"

"We want to make sure you're okay."

Stokes laughed. "As you can see, I'm fine. I'm just finishing some home improvements in the cellar. It's a mess down there so I'd like to get on with it if you don't mind."

He noticed the slight movement of their heads as they tried desperately not to look at each other. He'd seen that collusive look between them before.

"I think I'd like to take a look at that first." Ina pointed at his torso.

Stokes looked down. "It itches." He ran his finger around the edge. It took longer than he remembered, even longer than when Natalie Sutton had first created it with her double strike.

"It's growing," he added and looked up at them both.

He saw Ina swallow and wince before she took a step inside.

An enormous flash of pain ran through Stokes's entire body. It was worse than when the blade had crept below his flesh for the first time and this time it reached not only inside his body, but also his mind.

The room revolved around him and in an instant Ina and Peter were turned inside out. Their organs beat, pulsed and seeped in front of him and it was horrific. Ina took another step toward him.

"Jim, you need to let me help?"

He watched thick globules of blood drip from her outstretched fingers and land on the exposed floorboards.

"Keep back." He covered his eyes. "Stay away from me."

"It's okay, we'll help." Peter's voice echoed as if it was coming from the inside of a barrel.

"Stay away. Keep away from me." He could hear the throbbing rhythm of their hearts, the sloshing of their livers and the hissing of their kidneys and they were getting louder with each step. He could barely hear his own voice amid the cacophony.

Yet through it came the sound of a girl, a little girl screaming with all her might. "Keep them away from me, Daddy. Make them stay away."

It was too much. This was simply too much to bear. Any moment now he would fall to the ground as sure as if he'd been stabbed with a shiny steel blade. Any moment now he'd feel Natalie Sutton licking the back of his neck with her bloody tongue.

"Stop! All of you just stop. Leave me alone, please!" He opened his eyes and fell to the floor. Through a little crack in the boards he saw Melody looking up at him. She smiled and he passed out.

*

Something was trying to eat him from the inside, something with sharp teeth. It gnawed at his intestines and guts, slicing through them with difficulty, but cutting through eventually. The funny thing was, it didn't hurt quite as much as he imagined it might. In fact being eaten alive was probably an okay way to go if this was as bad as it got. He'd seen his dad eaten alive, not by a living creature but by cancer and that was about as far from okay as it was possible to be. No, this felt okay. Just wake me up when it's all over.

"I'll clean him up, you go back home and phone for an ambulance."

"Are you sure? I'm not sure I should leave you al…"

Stokes came to. The shouting and beating and hissing had stopped but it had left a dirty great scar running through the middle of his skull.

"What..?"

"Just sit still for God's sake."

He opened his eyes and looked down at Ina. She was kneeling in front of him. Thankfully her guts had been returned to the inside of her body. He was sitting on the recliner.

"I think I might be sick." He felt his stomach muscles spasm but the pain in his gut had lessened.

"Fetch a towel, Peter!"

Stokes heaved. It was a dry and rasping sound but it made his whole body convulse. There was nothing to bring up.

"Listen carefully, Jim. We need to get you to hospital and we need to get you there right now, okay?"

Stokes looked into her eyes. She was kind, they both were and he should listen to her, only the noises had started up again, faintly but they were there. Besides he'd been in the middle of something… something important.

"I was… I was about to…" What? What was he about to do?

"We know, you were about to make some improvements to the cellar, but they can wait. Believe me, they can wait." Peter loomed over him. The man was usually happy and gentle but there was something vaguely threatening about him.

"It won't wait," he muttered. Whatever it was.

"Pass me the sponge and then go." Ina held out her hand to Peter. The flesh on her fingers was gradually creeping back revealing beautifully clean and gleaming white bone underneath.

He handed her the sponge but didn't move. Ina held it up to Stokes. "I'm going to try my best to be gentle but if I catch you I'm sure you'll let me know."

She dipped it in the bowl by her side and squeezed off the excess water. He knew it was water, so why was it bright red?

"I hope you weren't saving this." She shuffled forward on her knees and started wiping his torso with the damp sponge. There was something vaguely sexual about the way she looked up at him. Something dirty. After only a couple of passes, she squeezed it into the bucket and started again.

"I need to…" Stokes started.

"I know," she replied and carried on.

What was it he needed to do? He looked at Ina and then at Peter. Their hearts were beating fast, faster than his own which pounded solidly in his chest. The skin on their faces looked wafer-thin and beneath the gossamer layer was a complicated-looking mess of ribbons and lines. It was like… like childish writing. What was written in there? He leaned forward. What was it?

"Now this might smart a little but we need to get the mud off." She turned sharply. "Peter, I asked you to go home and call for an ambulance."

"In a minute," he answered brusquely.

Ina squeezed the sponge out. "At least fetch some clean water before you go." She held the bowl out for him. He took it without a word and walked into the kitchen.

"Who did this to you?"

He looked down at the wound. "Natalie."

"Was she your wife?"

"Wife?" Stokes laughed. "Not exactly, she tried to kill me. She's dead."

"Did you kill her?" Peter placed the bowl on the floor beside Ina.

"Yes," he answered without pause. "I killed her the other night." He leaned forward slightly. "I slashed her to pieces, just like she tried to do to me."

He waited for the sharp intake of breath which surely must come after a disclosure like that but none came. Natalie had been dead long before he'd met her, she just hadn't realised it. Their meeting in the cellar was nothing more than the final straw in their doomed relationship.

"You haven't killed anyone, Jim." Ina patted the scar and he felt warm water trickle inside his body. It was a strange feeling but not unpleasant.

"Jesus." Peter's voice came through clenched teeth and it sounded like a hiss.

"Bad, isn't it?" Stokes winked at Peter. "I haven't had a really good look for a few days but it feels pretty grim."

He pulled himself a little more upright and examined it. There was a hole, there was nothing more to say about it than that, a hole somewhere between the size of a golf ball and a tennis ball. Ina's fussing had removed the grimy seal and a fresh and putrid stench rose from it. Peter held his nose and looked away.

"Never been to a post-mortem, have you?" He looked down at Ina again who, despite the stink, carried on cleaning him.

"That's what's happening here, a post-mortem." And it was. It was his own post-mortem and he had the best tickets in the house.

Ina pushed the sponge a little more vigorously against the edge of the hole, causing him to cry out.

"Just stop talking, Jim. This isn't a post-mortem." She half-turned to Peter, and shouted, "For God's sake, go!"

Her screech jarred Peter from his stunned silence and he jumped.

"Okay, okay, I'm going." He started for the patio doors but took one look back at Stokes as he passed.

"Compulsive viewing eh?" Stokes retched again.

"Teeth, there's teeth stuffed in there." Ina's voice stopped Peter in his tracks.

"What? What're you going on about?"

"Teeth, they're little teeth. Here, take a look." She moved to one side and Peter stepped forward cautiously. He stooped over and craned his neck.

Stokes roared with laughter. Both Ina and Peter were now stripped to the waist. Their insides were on show to him now. His little hole was nothing compared to how exposed they were.

"Jim?" He heard Ina's voice but he couldn't stop laughing.

"Oh shit." Peter sounded pathetic now.

"They're my mementos," Stokes managed to cough out.

A bomb detonated in his side and forced him forward. He needed to get out of this chair. He needed to get on with whatever he'd been doing before these two cretins had started interfering with him.

"Leave me alone!" he shouted and tried to stand.

Peter's hand pushed him back into the recliner.

"Look." Ina took her fingers out of the hole and offered one of the teeth up to Peter. Stokes saw his own blood hang limply from Ina's fingers before it fell into the water bowl.

"Put it back," he screamed. "Put it back, it's mine."

Another explosion of pain erupted as her fingers reached inside him again. "Where did these come from?"

Stokes tried again to force himself upright. He managed to bat away Peter's hand briefly before he was shoved back down again.

"They're mine, put them back inside me." He was

angry now. He turned to Peter. "You take your hand off me or I'll break it." He spat the words out.

"Where did you get them, Jim?"

Ina held the one she'd just extracted up to him. It was still as beautiful as ever.

"They're taking me away, bit by bit, tooth by tooth," Melody whispered into his ear. He could feel her breath on his flesh and it calmed him.

"I won't let them, sweetheart. I won't let them."

"What? Who are you talking to?" Ina was standing now but she held the tooth between her fingers and raised it to her eyes. She was fleshless down to her knees, they both were.

Stokes grabbed Peter's thumb and twisted it back and away with what little strength he still had. Peter stepped back and gave Stokes the opportunity to stand.

"Give it back, give them both back and leave." Were they still trying to help him? He really didn't know but if he didn't get what he wanted, he didn't care. He was having those teeth back and putting them where they belonged again. One way or another.

He took a step toward Ina who backed away. "Now." He spoke calmly but he was enraged.

He couldn't see Melody but she was there, right behind him. "They don't want to give them back. They want me for themselves but I want to stay with you. You'll look after me, won't you?"

"I will, I promise, don't worry."

He reached out to grab Ina's hand but Peter knocked it

away. Peter grunted and held his thumb close to his chest. The thumb wasn't broken but it was probably going to give him some grief for a while.

"I just want my things back, we both do. I'll hurt you again, Peter." He turned to Ina. "Both of you."

"Jim, this isn't right. You're ill." Peter walked to Ina's side. "You need the doctor."

Stokes stepped forward. "What I need is my things, they belong to…" He stopped.

"Who, Jim? Who do they belong to?" Ina stepped forward to meet him. Her voice was urgent.

"You'll have to take them, they won't give them back," Melody cried behind him.

He leapt forward and took hold of Ina's hand. A brief scuffle broke out with all three of them pulling at each other before Stokes fell back smiling. He had at least one of the teeth back. He stared at it for a moment and then ran it down his torso before pushing it inside the hole.

He cried out as he tried to push it back in but Ina had cleaned the wound so well that it wouldn't stick. The others had already been accepted by his body and had been absorbed into his flesh, or at least were starting to. He fumbled with it but his hands were slick with blood and it dropped to the floor. It wobbled for a second before dropping through a crack and falling into the cellar.

Stokes dropped to his knees and pounded the floor. "I'll kill you. I'll kill you both," he snarled.

He jumped up and flew at Peter, sending them both to the floor. Somewhere, someone was screaming and somewhere else, someone was laughing but he was too caught up in his own rage to know who was doing what.

He raised his fist and smashed it into Peter's gut. He heard Peter grunt as the wind was forced from his body. This rendered him completely vulnerable. Stokes crouched above him and raised his fist again. It didn't look like a human beneath him, it looked like a zombie or a science experiment. It wasn't a real person. But all those veins and arteries were pulsing and his voice was real.

"Do it, Daddy, do it again."

He'd heard similar words before. In a different life, when he'd been a detective and the lines were solid and unbroken, when he knew what he was doing.

"Do it!" Melody was standing beside him, looking down at the form which was somehow Peter Gauchment's face and body but couldn't have really been him.

"I can't Melody, I can't do it."

He rolled off Peter and looked up just in time to see the head of his own hammer an inch away from his face. As it hit his forehead, a bright flash of light sent a starburst across his eyes. The flash was accompanied by screaming, but this time there was no laughter. And then everything went black.

15

Willis came back from the brink slowly. There were people arguing above him. Was he in hell? If he was then he was exactly where he belonged. Stokes was mad, there was no doubt about that but he'd spoken about the girl. He'd said the name, Melody. He'd actually said her name. God, his face hurt and he could taste blood. He'd had a good beating but why wasn't he dead? He hadn't seen Stokes's eyes until they were on top of each other but the man had the look of someone for whom murder wouldn't be a leap, it would be the next and obvious step.

The voices above were familiar, too familiar…

*

"What have we done? What have you done?" Peter Gauchment collapsed onto the dirt and wailed.

"Her demons finally turned on her," Willis replied. "She must've…"

What? What exactly had her demons done to her?

Throttled her? No, that was down to him, a man of the cloth.

Kept her prisoner for an eternity until she'd actually become what they all feared? No, yet again that was him.

Turned their backs on her? No, no, no. That was all down to dear old mum and dad over there. One of them scratching around in the dirt like an animal and the other... Well, she was just as cool as ever. Mrs Perfect with her perfect Mother's Union smile and hand-knitted cardigan buttoned up to her outwardly-prudish neck.

"She must've had a heart attack or..."

"Well we can hardly call the coroner, can we?" There it was, that calmness that verged on disdain; an utter lack of empathy for her own daughter. Where did that come from? Who has that within them and still manages to behave like a normal human being?

He'd killed her. Even after she'd stopped choking and coughing he'd held onto her throat, squeezing and grimacing. Even after he'd known she was nothing more than a lifeless rag-doll, he'd squeezed her neck until the fragile bones crunched and creaked in the darkness.

He'd poured every single drop of self-loathing into the murderous act of strangulation. Each and every tormented suicidal thought had flowed through his fingers and into her body. It was as if his own twisted mind was killing her and not his hands. He squeezed until he could neither feel his arms or the delicate and broken neck of the little girl. And then he released her.

"Our daughter, this is our little Melody." He watched

Peter scoop the girl up in his arms. Her neck lolled to the side but the filth would hide the bruises. It would hide his fingerprints, engraved not only in the dirt, but in the soft flesh of her neck.

"Help me." He turned to his wife. It was a pathetic gesture but it went ignored. She simply stared at her husband.

"Help you do what, Peter? She's gone."

The torchlit incredulous look which spread across Peter Gauchment's face spoke of confusion, of pain and of hatred, of pure contempt for his wife. And then in the same instant they were all gone again as he looked down at the little girl in his arms.

"Help me?" He turned and looked directly at Willis. One man pleading with another for help when he has nowhere else to turn.

"We must bury her." It was all he could think to say. "We must bury her here."

"Like a dog? No, I shall take her to…"

"Peter, be quiet!" Ina's voice was loud yet controlled. "We must."

"You are a heartless creature and I hate you for it. I will always hate you."

For once he agreed with Peter. She was the most cold-blooded person he had ever met.

"I know. I have always known that, husband."

He watched Peter lower his daughter to the dirt and kiss her bald head.

"We're all in this together and we share an equal

portion of the blame. We will never speak about this again. We will never speak about her again. Peter and I are moving here soon and you'll be living here, Edward. We will forget." She turned to her husband. "We will all forget."

*

"We will forget," Willis mumbled into the darkness. "I have never forgotten."

The truth was that he had never been able to forget, even if he wanted to. He'd never quite been able to obliterate from his mind the crunch of her bones as he broke her neck. But there was something he'd seen in the dark voids of her eyes which had stayed with him through the sleepless nights in the psychiatric hospital… something far worse. He'd seen her soul and he'd seen the savage mess he'd made of it. A soul which should look like wispy clouds against a beautiful blue sky on a perfect summer's day looked like a sack of soot. And within that dirty, grimy bag was the face of a corrupt and faithless priest who thought more of his own salvation than that of a little girl. It was the last image she'd seen as he killed her.

"I'm sorry," he whispered and crawled to the place where they'd buried her. He gathered up a handful of the soil and held it to his mouth. His own soul was, at best, a sack of dog crap. He didn't deserve to be alive, none of them did.

Scretch, scretch, scretch.

Ah, she was here again.

"Is that you, Melody? Are you here?"

Scretch, scretch, scretch.

He pushed his hand against his lips and opened his mouth. Some of the looser soil fell into his mouth. A flesh-bag full of crap, that's all he was. He pushed more of the dirt into his mouth and tried to swallow. Rat shit was one stage lower than dog shit and that was what he deserved. He grabbed another fist full and forced it into his mouth. He bit down and felt his weak teeth buckle and snap as they hit a pebble. No matter, he would swallow them down too if he had to.

He heaved and coughed but he would complete this task. If Melody's soul was a dirty sack of soot then he would defile his own body and soul by this act of self-murder. If there had ever been any doubt about his next destination, this would seal the matter and ensure he would spend eternity lying in hell's cesspool.

Scretch, scretch, scretch.

He filled both hands with soil and crammed them greedily into his mouth. He coughed again but this time the cough didn't clear his throat, it couldn't. He gasped for air, he tried desperately to draw air into his lungs. Now the time was here and even though he wanted to kill himself and end his torment, something inside, something deep, deep down still clung to life. His arms reached forward but for what? There was nothing there, nothing except for a little girl coming out of the darkness toward him. She smiled and waved and he reached for her. Her smile was a picture, just like a girl he'd once known.

He tried to call out but there was no oxygen left in his body. It was her, it was Melody and she'd come to welcome him. Had he been wrong all along? Were his efforts to be rewarded?

She stepped forward. What was this? Where was the smiling little girl? Where had she gone?

Scretch, scretch, scretch.

Her mouth, her mouth? She wasn't smiling, was she? She was grinding her teeth together. Grinding them into sharp little points and showing them to him. And now she was coming toward him with those fangs showing and rats spilling from beneath her teeth, thousands and thousands of baby rats tumbling from her mouth and their teeth were like little needles.

This was wrong. It hadn't been his idea, it had been theirs, all theirs. He wanted to beg for forgiveness, he wanted to tell Melody that he'd only been trying to help her. He'd just lost his way somewhere along the line and… The first rats were upon him now, biting at his lips, forcing his gasping mouth wider and wider apart until they could climb inside him.

Then, as they descended deeper and deeper inside him, they gnawed and chewed at his guts, turning them to mush. The little girl looked down at him and laughed.

"Have you done the right thing, Vicar?"

Scretch, scretch, scretch.

She pulled two of her teeth out and rubbed them together. It was a lovely sound.

16

His body was being dragged across the dirt. Jagged little pebbles picked and nicked at his flesh but he barely felt them. He barely felt anything anymore, not even the gaping hole in his side.

Stokes opened his eyes but the skin on his face fought against the simple action. It felt like there was probably an ostrich-sized egg decorating his forehead.

There were candles in the cellar, or were they just painful impressions left by the hammer blow? The cellar looked more spacious under the candlelight but less friendly somehow. The way he felt at that moment, he didn't really care.

"Is that Willis?" He heard Peter's panic-stricken voice shaking.

"Yes," Ina answered bluntly.

My, she was a cold fish. When he'd first met Willis at the gathering, he'd said Ina was something else. He was right, she was as cold as ice.

They held a leg each and pulled him farther into the cellar.

"Is he okay? Did you know he was here?"

"He's dead, Peter. Now, don't you dare throw a wobbly on me just because the man you hate is dead. That would be hypocritical, wouldn't it."

There was silence for a moment before Peter spoke again. "Did Stokes kill him?"

"Probably." She was all business now. Gone was the Women's Institute poster girl and in her place was a cold-hearted monster.

Had he killed him? He remembered Willis coming into the cellar and the man grovelling in the dirt but he didn't recall killing the man. Had he wanted to, though? Things were all over the place now. Life and reality had become skewed.

He closed his eyes again and felt his body being pushed up against the wall, right next to Willis.

"Jesus, his mouth is crammed full of soil. It looks like he choked."

"Look like we've got an extra hole to dig then, doesn't it."

"Ina, we have to stop now. Things have gone too far."

"Too far? Things have gone too far? What about when you agreed to put your daughter in a hole, was that too far? What about when you said we ought to keep her down here until she wasn't a danger anymore, was that too far? Or how about when you helped dig her grave, just here? Was that too far, Peter? Was that too far!" Ina was clearly in charge and the rage in her voice illustrated it perfectly.

Peter groaned.

"We need do nothing. Willis broke in, a violent struggle ensued and Stokes killed him. Both of them were ill, Peter. Willis had a history of lunacy and this man, well I think the massive dose of blood poisoning will kill him soon anyway."

"Is he dead?"

Stokes felt a shove on his shoulder. He resisted it.

"No, but we can't just leave him here like this. We need to break his ankles so he can't move. The blood poisoning will do the rest."

Ah yes, that was what he'd been intending to do to Willis – hobble him. Smash his legs to bits for what he'd done to Melody.

"Melody?" He opened his eyes and shouted her name. She would come to him now. She would come and help him against…

"How do you know our daughter's name?" Ina looked into his eyes. Flames gathered in the corners of hers.

"Your daughter?" Stokes shook his head. "She calls me Daddy, she's my little girl."

A stinging slap jarred his head to the side, bumping it against Willis's shoulder.

"I'm her daddy!" Peter yelled.

A second slap jarred his head back the other way. "I'm her daddy!"

The candles were a horrible intrusion into the

comfortable darkness his eyes had grown accustomed to and they stung far more than the slaps. He closed his eyes again

"She's perfect." He smiled and licked his dry and cracked lips.

"How does he know her name?" Peter's voice had gone up a notch. "Tell me, dear wife, how the fuck this man knows my daughter's name?"

There was silence.

"I'm all ears."

"I… I don't know."

Ina grabbed Stokes's cheeks and squeezed them hard. "How?" she asked calmly and then more urgently. "Are you still a police officer?"

Stokes laughed and squinted. "Yeah, that's it, I'm an undercover copper and I've come to rescue Melody. I've come to rescue her like I did Natalie Sutton." He pointed to his stomach. "And look where that got me."

"Does he know?" He heard Peter shuffling his feet in the dirt.

"He doesn't know anything, you cretin."

"So how does he know her name, Ina? How does he know her name?" Peter was shouting now.

Scretch, scretch, scretch.

Stokes leaned forward, looked into Ina's burning eyes and whispered, "She's here."

One by one the candles were extinguished. Inch by inch the room grew dark and little by little Stokes began to see properly again.

He heard Ina and Peter gasp in unison.

"Melody?" he whispered.

She was standing in the far reaches of the room but it mattered not at all, for whether it was pitch black or whether it was noon in mid-summer it didn't matter, he could always see her. He knew he would always see her.

"Isn't she beautiful?" Stokes asked.

"What are you talking about? You're a lunatic, just like Willis." Peter was frightened, his voice was shaking almost to the point of being unintelligible.

"She's standing over there looking at you. She's looking right at you."

He heard the sound of shoes being shuffled in the dirt.

"Can't you see her? Just there, look." He pointed at Melody even though he knew they wouldn't see where he was pointing.

"They didn't want to see me again, that's why they locked me down here, with him."

"They're not your mummy and daddy, Melody. They don't deserve to be called that."

"She screamed when she saw me. The Vicar opened the hatch and she screamed when I looked up. She hates me."

"Then she's…" A blow caught him on his cheek. He'd been hit enough times to know this was a punch from someone unused to throwing a punch. Nevertheless it jarred his head to the side.

"Who are you talking to? Stop it, stop it now!"

"Peter! You're losing it. He's playing with us. There's no-one here except us three and a corpse."

Scretch, scretch, scretch.

Stokes snapped his head around sharply. Melody was standing right before him. She was so pretty, it was hard to imagine why anyone would want to lock her away. He reached out to touch her hair and to smell it again. He didn't need the moment of clarity her pure smell afforded him to know he was going to die and it was going to be sooner rather than later.

"I'm sorry I couldn't protect you. I'm sorry." A powerful wave of dizziness and nausea seized his body and threw him into a massive convulsion. It threw him forward and then at once, back again. He heaved and made a dry and terrible sound. If felt as if his organs were in their last throes and wanted to be free of his poisoned body.

He screamed in agony as wave after wave of excruciating agony ripped through his body. He wanted so much to open his eyes, just to look at her before it all ended, but he was afraid to. What if she was just a dream? A beautiful and sad dream that his destroyed mind had conjured up to save him.

He screamed again and tasted blood in his mouth.

"I'm sorry, Melody." He opened his eyes and smiled. She was still there, standing in front of him with her hands reaching out toward his body, reaching toward his torso. In bright red letters scrawled across her forehead was the word 'Dead'.

"It's written across my face too, isn't it?" His words didn't feel right as they formed on his lips. They were numb and without clarity. They were bubbling through blood, lots of blood.

Melody reached inside him and touched her teeth.

"I've kept them safe for you." He slumped forward.

Scretch, scretch, scretch.

17

She watched from across the room as they dragged the nice daddy across the dirt. He was sick, really sick and she'd seen people like that before. She'd seen the colour of the writing in their skin and it wasn't a good colour. His mind had gone bad long before she'd shown herself to him, before she'd been allowed to show herself to him. There had been someone else in there, a really nasty someone who wouldn't leave him alone. Her name was Natalie. She didn't know who she was but her name was printed in capital letters across his entire body. Big, black capital letters and they dripped with an oozing oil that was poisonous.

Natalie, whoever she was, had been pushed deep, deep down inside him on the night he'd come to the cellar with a knife. He could never get rid of her completely, she was as much a part of him as the hole in his stomach and the little shiny jewels in the hole.

He wasn't well then and he'd only got worse and

worse. She was sad about that because he wasn't a nasty man like the Vicar and he certainly wasn't like Daddy, the real daddy. Mummy was cruel too – she'd screamed when the Vicar opened the hatch and nearly blinded her. That was a horrible thing to do. It was mean.

"Melody?"

They were hitting him now and Daddy was screaming. She could see in the dark better than they could, even better than the nice man.

"I'm here, Daddy." She called over to him. She couldn't go any closer yet. What if they saw her again and screamed? She couldn't bear to go through that again.

The nice daddy pointed at her. He wanted her to come over. He wanted her help.

"They didn't want to see me again, that's why they locked me down here, with him."

"They're not your mummy and daddy, Melody. They don't deserve to be called that."

"She screamed when she saw me. The Vicar opened the hatch and she screamed when I looked up. She hates me."

She felt a terrible sense of losing something creep through her body again. She didn't want to feel like this anymore. She didn't want to. She wouldn't.

She pulled two of her teeth out, rubbed them together and moved toward them all.

Scretch, scretch, scretch.

He was close to the edge. What the edge truly was she didn't quite know, but she was standing on it all the time and she knew if she allowed herself to fall off it, that would be it. That would be the end and she'd have to leave the cellar for ever. She didn't want that, she didn't want to leave. Ever.

He looked in lots of pain and the blood which ran from his mouth was the same colour as the dirt inside the rat's nest.

He kept saying sorry. He kept saying he was sorry to her and that he couldn't protect her. He shouldn't be sorry. No, he was giving her exactly what she'd always wanted from him. She reached out and felt her fingers slip inside the hole in his tummy. That was where the jewels were, that was where her treasure was kept and it was where she was going.

The nice daddy slumped over. Immediately his body was covered in a thousand words. It was the same word over and over and over again and it was in bright white writing.

Dead.

She touched the teeth buried deep inside his dead body and felt a tingle pass along her fingertips. She wriggled deeper and deeper into him until she couldn't see herself anymore, until his body yielded to her completely. His death had given her new life. It was exactly what she wanted and now she had a real body again, she intended to make up for lost time.

"You look much older now." They were her words but it wasn't her voice, it was his. It didn't matter as long as they listened.

"What?" Mummy was looking at her with a strange

look on her face.

"I said you look much older now, than the last time I saw you that is. I think that was when you took me out of my bed and put me in his car." She raised an arm that also didn't belong to her and pointed at the Vicar.

"He brought me here and you let him keep me locked away."

Mummy looked a little bit scared. That was good, that was how it was supposed to be.

"You shut your mouth." Daddy came toward her with his hand raised to hit her, but in the darkness his aim was bad and his punch glanced across the nice daddy's cheek.

"Hello Daddy." She raised an arm and swept it into Daddy's face. She heard him gasp and fall to the ground. "I can see you're afraid. It's easy to see."

"Peter, can't you see he's playing with us. It's just Stokes…"

She shuffled forward. Changes were happening inside the nice daddy's body, they were just like the ones she'd felt after the Vicar had put his hands around her neck and squeezed.

"You would only look at me at bed-time when the lights were out and it was dark. When you thought I was asleep and I couldn't see you when I couldn't see what was written on your face. Can you remember that, Daddy?"

She stamped on his fingers as he grovelled in the dirt.

"I can see quite well in the dark now. I can see how afraid you are. You've always been afraid of me, haven't you?"

Daddy was very afraid now. He turned his head to look at her but there was no recognition in his eyes, there was nothing in his eyes but there was plenty going on in his head.

"It's me, Daddy. It's your little girl." She raised a boot and brought it down on his face. There was a terrible yet wonderful sound of cracking teeth as the boot connected. She reached down and scooped the fragments up. She had the perfect place set aside for them, right next to her own. She would remove all of his teeth after she'd had a little chat with Mummy.

"All of my hair and all of my teeth fell out. Is that why you screamed when you saw me?" She looked at Mummy who looked like she was still in control. She had always been in control.

"Melody?" Her voice didn't break but it caught on the way out, just a little, just enough to be heard by the rats.

"Yes, it's me. Why, Mummy? Why?"

"Why?"

"Why did you stop loving me?" That's all that mattered. Why had they stopped loving her?

"We never stopped loving you. This was never meant to happen but..." Her voice trailed off.

Melody forced her feet to move forward. "I cried. I cried all the time. I cried until there were no more tears in my body. I was so sad I wanted to die but you never came to see me, neither of you."

"I heard you, I felt every single tear but I couldn't come." Mummy was still in control.

Melody took another step forward until their feet were touching. She was getting angry. "Why?" she demanded.

"Do you know what the girls in school used to call me, Melody?"

Melody shook her head.

"They said I was a witch."

"Why?"

"We're the same, Melody. I can see people's feelings and what their soul says, just like you. I see the same way you do."

She could see the same way? She could see what people thought, what they were feeling, just the same.

"You are a liar." She clenched her fist and struck Mummy across the face. It felt good.

"I know what you want. I can see it clearly. It's written through your core, Melody."

"And what's that, Mummy?"

"You want love, you want Daddy and me to wrap our arms around you and hold you like we did when you were tiny. That's what you want, Melody."

Is that what she wanted? Is that all she'd ever wanted?

She leaned in close. There was someone inside Jim's head that needed to get out. Someone who'd been waiting for only a short time but who had a lifetime of pain to inflict on someone, on anyone.

"Mummy, I'd like you to meet a friend of Jim's, she's called Natalie."

Melody gripped her mother's head and peered into her eyes. She'd seen Natalie pecking at Jim's brain for the last week and now she could feel her in there, scratching and nibbling. She wasn't real, not like her anyway, she was just something his poorly brain had created. She was one of those monsters that only came out at night. They were the worst kind but they weren't real and Natalie only existed inside Jim's mind. She wasn't anywhere else, not like her.

Jim wasn't in charge of his mind now, she was, and she could send Natalie to her mummy, wrapped up just like a gift. Natalie was ready to belong to someone else now.

Mummy didn't like what she could see in there, in Jim's eyes, and she tried to back away but he was strong, too strong and she couldn't go anywhere.

"She's nasty, really nasty." She felt the object of Jim's imagination creep forward. Her wild hair swept behind her like a filthy cloud and her wild eyes spoke of only one thing – madness. She lived only inside Jim's head but that was enough.

"What do you see, Mummy? What do you see in me now?"

The room was ablaze for less than a second but in that brief moment Melody felt the strength in Jim's legs give way. Mummy fell back against the wall.

The words came thick and fast as they were tattooed into her skull, her brain and her skeleton. There were words she couldn't understand, words she had seen before and ones which she had never wanted to see. They were the words of a vicious lunatic created in a mind so damaged that it had destroyed itself. Jim's mind had created the perfect monster, and it had been crafted with one purpose – to push someone over the edge and into an abyss from which there can be no escape.

"Can you see them, Mummy? Can you feel them? Now you can really see just like me." She laughed and picked up a handful of dirt. She hadn't felt the soil on her fingers for a very long time. It was cool and damp, just like it had always been. The sharp pebbles and stones which ran through it had caused terrible injuries to her toes at first.

Her hand closed around a rock the size of her own skull. As a little girl she had barely been able to pick rocks of this size up. Jim was much stronger and even though he was fading fast, it felt as light as a feather.

She looked at Mummy, the woman who'd called herself Mummy for a few years anyway. She lay there, staring into the darkness, twitching and licking her lips.

"We've not quite finished yet, Mummy." She got to her feet slowly, clutching the large rock in one hand and reaching inside what was left of Jim Stokes with the other.

She pulled out the jagged shards of her teeth and turned to Daddy.

"The same goes to you too, Daddy. I've got something left to say."

Scretch, scretch, scretch.

*

She stumbled across the dirt toward the hatch. There wasn't much time left now. She could feel him seeping away bit by bit, drifting out and away, just like she'd done.

214

It was just like she'd tried to do but something had been tied around her ankles, which tethered her to the cellar like a balloon. She'd got those things now, she'd put all her teeth right back where they were supposed to be – inside the little box of treasures.

She pulled Jim's body up into the house. The light was blinding but it felt good on his skin. It soothed him inside. He'd died in the cellar with that horrible Natalie still floating around in his skull but she'd taken her out and given her to Mummy. And now that Mummy was dead, she'd have to keep Natalie with her for the rest of time.

She stood and looked out of the window. All this time she'd been in the house, she'd never seen what was on the outside. A few ducks waddled in the water just below the house and in the distance, just across the lake, a group of trees were swaying in time with the breeze. It was beautiful.

She sat down by the window and looked at her hands. There was no skin visible anymore, just thick, dark blood. She lay back and crossed her hands over Jim's chest. He didn't deserve to be found down there with them. Besides, when the last of him went wherever it was destined to go, she didn't want anything tethering him to the house. He was better than that.

She closed her eyes and felt the last of him go.

She fell from his body and slipped through the boards, back to the darkness she loved; back to see Mummy and Daddy.

18

C.S.I. Cunningham packed away the scene lights and sat on the case. He needed a drink and he needed one now. He'd been drinking a lot recently, too much and it was fast becoming a spiteful little habit. He popped a mint into his mouth and licked his lips. As far as scenes went this was an absolute beauty, probably a once in a lifetime job, but all he could think about was that drink.

The ex-detective found by the window upstairs was the start but none of the uniform boys had expected to find the other three in the cellar. The dead copper had got a hole in his guts so deep you could see part of his spine. He never got sick at the sight of human atrocity anymore but the whole place smelled of death. He'd once been called to a house where two brothers had killed each other, but as soon as he'd come inside this place he knew there was more than two dead bodies in here. A house didn't smell this bad for no good reason.

He'd photographed them all in situ and then

individually from every angle imaginable. Two of the major crime boys had come out of the cellar retching at the moment he'd been photographing the detective. It had made him smile. All that bravado counted for nothing when you were faced with human beings whose heads had literally been smashed into fragments. There were things you couldn't un-see.

They were taken away, one by one. One man had a windpipe so full of dirt they'd need a pneumatic drill to unblock it. He was lucky.

The level of violence used on the other two was unparalleled in his experience and certainly in the experience of the young DI. The scene lights had lit up drops of blood on his lower lip as he chewed it furiously. It wasn't as if they could be identified from dental records either. They didn't have any teeth left.

They were covered in writing, that's what really messed with the Inspector's hypothesis. What was all that writing for? The vicar was covered in it too.

Writing wasn't quite correct though, was it. Tattooing?

Etching probably came closer to the truth. The bodies of the two, one male and one female, had been etched with bloody writing. It was clear a knife hadn't been used, the letters had been ground into the skin, not cut and not sliced. No, it had been something sharp and probably jagged. Something like…

He shuffled his boots in the dirt. Something like a precious stone, a gem perhaps. He stooped and used his fingers like forceps to pick it up. He rolled it using his thumb and forefinger. It was perfect, so clean and…

"Ouch." A little bead of blood pooled in the tip of his thumb. Surface tension gave it flawlessly smooth and rounded edges. If you had enough time it might do the job but it was too small, far too small. Nevertheless it was beautiful. He slipped it inside his pocket.

The DI had closed the scene down yesterday but it would be a long time until this mess was concluded, if ever.

How long must it have taken for someone to etch that much graffiti into the flesh of three people? A day? Two perhaps. The word 'dead' had been scrawled into their foreheads in capital letters and the marks ran the deepest of all. The word was probably superfluous given the circumstances.

But the others, what were they supposed to infer? Were they accusations?

Murderer, adulterer, weak, cuckold, faithless, hate, fear, spite, witch. The words went on and on and on but none of them had good connotations. Someone didn't have much time for these three. The ex-detective with blood poisoning on a colossal scale would probably be made to wear this one in the report but that didn't feel quite right. It didn't fit.

Besides, the child's bones they'd found pre-dated him by several years. He hadn't put them down there, that was for absolute sure.

Cunningham stood up and rubbed his eyes. It would be nice to get back up into the light again. Back into the world of the living, so to speak. It would be good to get away from the rats and their infernal scratching too. He hadn't seen any, thank God, but there had to be a nest down here from all the noise they were making.

Scretch, scretch, scretch.

He picked up the final case and headed for the hatch. None of the others had wanted to stay down here any longer than was necessary but it wasn't all that bad once you got used to it. He pushed the case through the gap and patted his pocket. Even in the gloom of the cellar the little gem had looked stunning, but he'd take it back home and have a look at it in the daylight. It was perfect.

"Goodbye, rats!"

He climbed up and looked out onto the lake. Given the history of the place, he might be able to pick it up for next to nothing at an auction.

Scretch, scretch, scretch.

He sunk his hand into his pocket and touched the little jagged jewel. He'd have to get rid of the rats though. They sounded like they were upstairs too, they sounded like they were everywhere.

Scretch, scretch, scretch.

The End

12188218R00132

Printed in Great Britain
by Amazon.co.uk, Ltd.,
Marston Gate.